HER STERN COWBOY

RENEE MARKS

Published by Blushing Books
An Imprint of
ABCD Graphics and Design, Inc.
A Virginia Corporation
977 Seminole Trail #233
Charlottesville, VA 22901

Renee Marks
Her Stern Cowboy

ebook ISBN: 978-1-64563-721-9
Print ISBN: 978-1-64563-722-6
Audio ISBN: 978-1-64563-723-3
v1

Chapter 1

"**O**h come on, Lily, what's the matter, sweetheart? You've been fed, changed, had your bottle, it's time to go to sleep, everything's okay." Andrea Malone tried to soothe her long-time best friend's eight-month-old little girl. She bounced her in her arms gently, not understanding what was going on. She had never acted like this before. Nothing seemed to be appeasing the blonde hair cutie.

Andrea was almost at her wits end when her phone began to make a high-pitched ringing noise. Who would be calling at two a.m.? Maybe Candice and her husband Caleb had decided to pick Lily up. She rushed to her room with the squirming, upset baby in her arms and got to her phone just before it went to voicemail. "Hello?"

"Andrea Malone?" a woman's voice questioned.

"Yes, this is she, can I help you?" she answered, struggling to hold the phone and Lily.

"I know this is an ungodly hour and it sounds like the baby is upset but I need you to come down to the station, ma'am," the woman continued.

"Station? What are you talking about?" Andrea was so confused as she tried to get Lily to settle down.

"Yes, ma'am, the Whitehorse Police Station. You are in Whitehorse, correct, ma'am?"

"Yes, but what's going on?" Andrea was becoming more confused and she was beginning to get scared.

"I'll explain when you get here, ma'am. Ask for Detective Murphy when you come in, please."

"O-o-okay," Andrea stuttered and ended the call. Panic seized her as she got Lily dressed and then her own daughter Lucy, who was ten months old. She made sure their diaper bags were ready and they headed out to the car.

She placed Lily and Lucy both in their car seats and began the short trip to Whitehorse Police Department, even though it felt like it was taking forever. What on Earth happened?

Andrea finally pulled in to the parking lot and found a spot relatively close to the door. After exiting the car, she took Lucy out and then Lily while still in her carrier. She walked toward the door, one carrier in hand, two diaper bags around her shoulders and another baby on her hip.

She had to look a sight, she hadn't even taken the time to change out of her baggy t-shirt, black tight shorts and flip-flops. She was sure her hair was a mess and she felt like she was going to keel over from lack of sleep.

She found a very thin, blonde woman sitting behind a desk. Andrea walked up to her quickly and said, "Excuse me, I'm supposed to ask for a Detective Murphy."

The woman seemed to scrutinize her for a moment then replied, "Give me a few minutes, ma'am. I'll let Detective Murphy know you're here." She got up from the desk and left, leaving Andrea there by herself with two upset kids and looking like hell.

She glanced around at the mostly empty station, she noticed a couple of chairs that were free, they didn't look too comfy, but it was better than nothing. She took a seat as Lily began to cry again.

Andrea set the carrier and diaper bags down. She sat Lucy in the other chair for a minute, unhooked Lily from the car seat, pulled her up against her shoulder and rocked her back and forth while Lucy climbed in her lap.

"I know, Lil, shh, I know you're so tired, I just wish you'd stop fighting it ." Andrea tried to soothe her as Lily rubbed her eyes then tried to push away from Andrea.

"Ms. Malone?" a female voice called out. Andrea stood with the two girls held tightly in her arms.

"Yes?"

"Oh, wow, I didn't know you had two children with you."

"Um yeah, I'm watching one for my best friend," Andrea explained as she adjusted both girls and Lily rubbed her snotty nose against her t-shirt.

"Now I wish someone else would have answered my call," the woman said as she stepped forward and reached to take Lucy.

Andrea let her, the woman was a police officer after all. Andrea picked up the diaper bags and carrier, adjusted Lily in her arms as she squirmed again, and followed the officer to another room which was quiet and secluded. It looked a lot more comfortable than the waiting room she'd been in.

"Are you Detective Murphy?" Andrea managed to ask as she set the bags on the long dark table and the carrier on the floor.

"Yes, ma'am. Is this little one I'm holding yours?"

"Yes, she is, that's Lucy. Will you please explain to me why I'm here at almost three in the morning?" Andrea asked and adjusted Lily again. She reached to take Lucy but Detective Murphy shook her head.

"I don't mind holding her, she seems more relaxed than

Lily. Is it okay if I hold her for a little bit? You're new here aren't you?"

"Sure, you can hold her, thanks. And yes, I moved out here shortly before I had Lucy, I wanted to be closer to my best friend, Candice."

"Ms. Malone, I'm so sorry to tell you this, and I don't know any easy way to tell you, but Candice and Caleb were killed last night. We suspect a robbery, their wallets, jewelry, and anything else valuable were taken from them. The only reason we know who they were... well, it's a small town," Detective Murphy explained.

Andrea just stared at the detective, everything felt like it was moving in slow motion. Caleb and Candice were gone? A robbery? In this small town? Why?

"Ms. Malone, are you still with me?" Detective Murphy asked.

Andrea's gray eyes met the detective's green-brown eyes. "What? I'm sorry. Are you sure?"

Detective Murphy adjusted Lucy. "We tried to call all of their family, but no one answered but you, we need you to identify them. We'll do everything in our power to find who did this, they were great people."

"What about Lucy and Lily? I can't leave them," Andrea whispered as tears began to fill her eyes. Her best friend was gone, what was she going to do?

"I'll have a couple officers come in and take care of them while I take you to the morgue."

Andrea flinched a little at the word morgue. "Can't... can't you wait to get a hold of one of their family members? I don't think I can do it."

"We've already tried again, and we waited at least four hours before we called you. I'm sorry I can't make this painless."

Andrea saw the compassion in the detective's green-brown

eyes. She finally took the rest of her in, brown wavy hair, a warm skin tone and petite. Andrea choked back a sob. "Okay," she said and sighed in defeat.

"All right, I'll be back with a couple of officers to watch the babies."

Andrea nodded her head. She had no clue what was in store for her, twenty-five years old and she never once had to identify a body. She shivered at the thought but tried to keep the tears at bay. She had to do this.

───────

Elijah Cameron woke up to the four a.m. alarm. Ranching started early. He turned the alarm off and rolled out of bed. He checked his phone like every morning. Four missed calls and two voicemails.

He frowned, that was rare. He looked at the number but he didn't recognize it. He dialed his voicemail and listened to the two messages. Both were from the Whitehorse Police Department. What the hell? He called them back and asked for Detective Murphy as the message instructed.

"I'm so sorry, Mr. Cameron, she's currently with someone. But I'm sure she would want you to come down here, there's been an accident but that's all I can tell you over the phone, you should get here as quickly as you can."

"Okay, I'll be there soon," he replied and hung up, forgetting the shower. He threw on his dark jeans and a white T-shirt, headed downstairs and pulled on his dark brown, worn boots. He grabbed his keys and brown Stetson then headed out the door.

He shot a text to a couple of the guys who showed up early to let them know where he went and that he'd be back soon.

He jogged over to his gray two-fifty super duty and headed into town.

A million thoughts ran through his mind as he rushed to the police station. What kind of an accident? Who was involved? His heart began to race as he made the drive. He pulled out his phone to call his big brother but it went straight to voicemail. Odd.

Andrea jumped when the door opened again. She looked up to see Detective Murphy usher in two male officers.

Andrea felt unsure at first, the feeling must have been written all over her face.

"It's okay, Ms. Malone. This is Officer Dean and Officer Carl, they're fathers and know how to handle children well," Detective Murphy explained.

Andrea let out a sigh and began to get up, kissing both girls she said, "I'll be right back, sweeties." Lucy and Lily both grabbed for her and it broke her heart not being able to take them.

She followed Detective Murphy down the skinny hallway to a door. Murphy turned toward her and squeezed her arm. Andrea locked eyes with the woman.

"I know this is going to be hard but I will not leave your side," the detective assured.

Andrea took a deep breath and nodded her head. She just wanted to get this done and go home. She was exhausted, the girls were exhausted and she just wanted to be able to let all the emotions out.

They walked into the room, she felt an instant chill crawl along her exposed skin. She wrapped her arms around herself tightly, letting her body shiver. Everything sent her reeling. One wall was completely bare, the other wall was metal and had small metal doors. She took a deep, uncalming breath as Detective Murphy walked up in between two doors.

"Okay, I know this is going to be difficult."

"Just do it," Andrea gritted out between clenched teeth, no matter how much they talked it wasn't going to change anything and wasn't going to prepare her. She tried to prepare herself a little better as the detective opened the first drawer, a sheet covered the body.

The detective slowly pulled the sheet back, there lay Caleb Cameron. He was so pale, so lifeless. Tears blurred her vision as she looked away from him quickly. "Yeah, that's Caleb," she choked out.

Murphy pushed the table back in and closed the door. She stepped back to move to the next door beside where Caleb's body lay. She slowly pulled the table out and lowered the other sheet.

The tears fell. "That's Candice." Andrea couldn't believe what she was looking at. Her best friend of twenty years lying there pale, lifeless just as Caleb was.

Andrea turned away quickly and rushed out of the cold room. She couldn't find the bathroom, she rushed out the front door and lost everything she had eaten earlier.

She collapsed to her knees as she cried. She held her stomach tightly as she knelt there crying.

Elijah was standing in front of the receptionist at the police department and chatting with her a little, waiting for Detective Murphy to show up.

All of a sudden he heard the sound of pounding footsteps. His head jerked up and he saw the short spitfire he couldn't mistake. Andie Malone, Candice's best friend.

He watched her take off out the door and fall to the ground. He took off after her and heard the gut-wrenching sound of her getting sick and the tears. He crouched down behind her a little, "Andie, what's wrong?" he asked calmly.

She turned toward him a little. Her beautiful gray eyes were wide in shock and tears profusely spilled down her cheeks.

"Oh, Eli," she sobbed out but apparently couldn't say anything else.

Elijah didn't know what to do, he pulled her little body back against his huge one. "Calm down and talk to me, Andie."

She shook her head quickly then began to pull away from him. "I have to get the girls," she whispered.

"Lucy and Lily?" Eli asked gently.

She nodded and stood up, stumbling a little.

He reached out and caught her, her body felt so cold. "Andie?" he questioned as the door behind him opened.

"Ms. Malone," Detective Murphy called out. "Oh, thank goodness, you're still here, the babies are crying. I tried and so did Officer Dean and Officer Carl, we just can't get them to calm down."

Andie pulled away from Eli and headed back inside. She seemed so dazed and confused. Eli followed her inside and Detective Murphy followed behind him.

"Eli, can we talk for a minute?"

Eli sighed as he watched Andie rush away. He couldn't believe she was only wearing booty shorts, flip-flops, and an old t-shirt. She should have known better than to wear something like that.

He heard a throat clear and he turned back to the detective. "What happened, Murphy?" he demanded almost glaring at her.

"There was an incident with Caleb and Candice, no one but Ms. Malone answered, we found her in recent messages and knew she had Lily. Eli, they were robbed and we believe there was a struggle. Caleb and Candice, both of them are gone. Eli, I'm so sorry."

"What?" he gasped out as he stumbled down into a chair.

"Eli, knowing Caleb he fought the perp off, but they were shot," Murphy explained trying to meet his eyes.

He looked away to back down the hall. "So what did you need Andie for?"

"She was the last one we called, we didn't know she had a daughter as well, we only knew she was watching Lily, we needed someone to confirm who we had here," Murphy explained.

"Out of everyone you had to drag her down here to identify who's lying in the morgue? Well, I'm here now, so let's do this." Anger filled him, how dare Murphy pull Andie into this. She wasn't even family. She was the best friend of his sister-in-law.

"She already did," Murphy whispered.

Eli was up out of the chair in an instant, no wonder she was such a wreck. "Where is she?" he demanded, his temper flaring even more. He always was the one who had a short fuse, Caleb had always been the calm one.

"Second door on the right," Murphy answered.

He took off to the door she directed him to, he pushed it open and couldn't believe it when he saw Andie trying to console both her daughter and his niece. "Andie, here let me," he took Lucy who was closer to him and began to bounce her up and down while Andie dealt with Lily. "Come on, let me get you girls home."

Andie looked up at Eli, she frowned a little when she met his amber eyes, they were more coppery right now, "Just help me get them to the car, I can handle everything else."

"Andie, I can help," Eli tried again.

She shook her head. "No, I'll handle it," she said icily. She learned a while ago not to trust men. Not to depend on them. And this cowboy would be no different.

"I can call my mom, she'll take Lily," he offered.

"No, she still needs to be told with a chance to acknowledge it, Eli. Not be told then adding 'hey take care of your granddaughter'. It's fine, Eli, I can handle it." She placed a now calm Lily in her carrier, grabbed the bags and rushed out of the room. She made her way to her candy blue Camry with Eli right behind her.

She placed Lily in the car and buckled the carrier down, then took Lucy and walked around the other side of the car and placed the miniature her in the other carrier.

She got in the driver's side and went to start the car. She had to get away from Eli, away from the police station. She just wanted to be home.

She heard a knock on her window which made her jump. She looked over and Eli was standing there. She closed her eyes tightly but put her window down. "What, Eli?"

"Do you have my number?" he asked as he leaned down in the window, which couldn't be easy with him being over six feet tall.

"No, I don't, Eli. You know I don't." She sighed feeling exasperated, they never got to know each other over the last year that she'd been here. So when would they have ever exchanged numbers?

"Phone," he demanded holding out his huge hand toward her.

She narrowed her eyes at him, refusing to look into his eyes. She grabbed her phone from the front seat and handed it to him. "I don't know why we have to do this, Eli."

"Because you shouldn't be alone during this, so if you need

me or anyone just call." He finished putting his number in her phone and handed it back to her.

She'd just delete it later, she thought, as she took the phone and threw it in the seat beside her again.

"I'm serious, Andie, I'll check on you later. I'll talk to Mom and Dad, see how they want to handle all of this. I don't want to ask but can you call Candice's family and let them know?" He squeezed her shoulder.

Tears began to fill her eyes. "Yeah, I'll handle it."

"Thanks, Andie."

"Can I go now?"

"Yeah."

She waited for him to step back from the car before she backed out and began to head home. She had just pulled into the driveway as both girls began to cry again. She closed her eyes tightly, looked like she wasn't opening her bakery today. It didn't matter it was right beside her house.

There was just no way. She got out of the car, got the babies and bags out, then headed to the small two-bedroom gray house. She laid them both down on the floor in the living room near their toys and began to prepare their bottles.

Lucy seemed to calm down once she was out of the seat but poor Lily wasn't having any part of calming down.

Andie rushed to her and began to feed her first. The poor little girl knew something was wrong.

Andie let out a sigh of relief as Lily began to eat. Once she was done, Andie changed her diaper then laid her down in the play and pack as she finally began to fall asleep, over exhausted.

She did the same with Lucy and laid her in the play and pack also. She pulled out her phone and called Mrs. Howell, Candice's mother.

Mrs. Howell answered on the third ring. "Andrea, have you heard from Candice? I cannot get a hold of her."

Andie bit back the tears. "That's why I'm calling, Mrs. Howell. I don't want to do this over the phone but if you're not sitting down, Mrs. Howell, I think you should," Andie said.

"Andrea, dear, you're scaring me but I'm sitting down."

"Mrs. Howell, Caleb and Candice were involved in a robbery, they were shot late last night. They... um... they didn't make it. They're both gone," Andie barely got the words out before the tears started again.

"Oh my God! The baby?"

"She's with me, I've had her since last night. Caleb and Candice were having their weekly date night," Andie explained.

"Oh my God, Bruce and I will come out right away. Are you okay, Andie?"

"Yeah, I'll be fine. I've got two little girls to take care of at the moment, they come first," she whispered into the phone.

"We'll be there soon, sweetie." Mrs. Howell hung up the phone.

Andie threw her phone on the other side of the couch and checked on the girls to make sure they were still okay. She lay down on the couch and curled up into a ball as she stared blankly at the wall. She felt so numb, she hadn't felt this numb in her life. What was she going to do now?

Chapter 2

Eli sat in his parents' driveway, he was a little upset that Andie wouldn't let him help her. But could he really blame her with the way she was left by her ex after finding out she was expecting Lucy? He let out a sigh. His brother was always telling him about Andie, even though he had never once asked about her. They had danced at Candice and Caleb's wedding once when it was time for the wedding party to dance and he walked her up and down the aisle since she was the Maid of Honor and he had been the Best Man. That was as far as it could have gone.

What was he thinking? That woman shouldn't be invading his mind at all right now. His brother was gone. So was his sister-in-law. And now he had to go break the news to his parents.

Once they figured out arrangements they would handle what happened to Lily. He got out of his truck and headed up to the red brick house.

He knocked on the dark green door. He shoved his hands in his day-old jeans fighting the anger that threatened him. He needed a calm, cool, and collected head right now.

The door opened and he was staring down at his mother's five-two frame, with some wrinkles and flecks of gray through her dark black hair and expressive green eyes.

"Elijah, what on earth are you doing here? Come in, come in." She stepped aside and he walked into the tiny one-bedroom, one-bathroom house they had moved into a few years back.

"Hi, Mom, is Dad home?"

"Yes, he's in the kitchen, we were just getting ready to eat breakfast." She began to go toward the little tan kitchen.

"Can we talk in the living room?" His deep voice actually broke a little.

Maisy Cameron turned back to her son. "Is everything okay?" Worry etched itself on her face in an instant.

He took a deep breath and shook his head a little. "Just get Dad, please." He yanked his Stetson off and raked his fingers through his blond hair. He turned away quickly and headed to the living room.

He sat on the coffee table as he waited for his parents.

"I don't know, Todd, something is very wrong though, please hurry." Eli heard the worry in his mom's voice and his dad grumbling a little.

He sat there his head hung low, clutching his hat. How were they going to get through this? Then again, they had to for Lily's sake.

He glanced up as they came into the living room. "Please, sit." He motioned to the brown leather couch he was sitting across from. As they sat his amber eyes darted from his mom's worried filled eyes to his dad's own amber eyes. He slowly looked back down at the ground.

They both were getting up there in age a little, his dad had some wrinkles but you couldn't make out any gray on him due to having light blond hair.

The two Cameron sons took after their father, Todd Cameron, there was no mistake about that.

"Eli?" his mother's voice shattered his thoughts and he snapped his head back up.

Never show defeat, he told himself. "Mom, Dad, something happened last night. Did you not have missed calls on your phones this morning?"

"We haven't turned them on yet," Maisy began. "We turn them off at night and then turn them on in the morning after breakfast."

Eli rolled his eyes to himself, parents. "Whitehorse Police Department called, I had four missed calls and two voicemails from them when I woke up this morning. There was an incident with Caleb and Candice, they went out on their weekly date night last night. Apparently someone tried to rob them, it didn't go as planned I assume, Caleb probably scuffed with the perp, they shot him." He closed his eyes tightly. "And Candice, they're gone," he whispered, then opened his eyes to look at his parents.

They sat there wide-eyed in shock. "Lil?" Todd shot out finally.

"Andie has her, Candice's friend, she always watches Lil on their date night. Don't start anything yet, let's get the arrangements made then we will figure out what is going on with Lily. They got a hold of Andie this morning, she was the only one who answered the phone call, she had to identify Caleb and Candice."

"Oh, that poor girl, is she okay?" Maisy asked.

"She was pretty shaken up when I got to the station, but she seemed to pull herself together pretty quickly once she thought of the girls," Eli managed to answer.

Maisy broke down in tears as Todd wrapped his arms around her tightly.

Eli laid his hands on each one of their knees. He'd only

been good at showing his anger, but right now he didn't know how he felt. "Andie called Candice's parents to let them know. I have to go check on the ranch, see that everyone is doing their jobs and tell them all what's going on."

Maisy and Todd nodded their heads. "Once we find out about Candice's family we'll do the funeral and everything."

"Okay, I'll try to find out things from Andie later, she looked pretty drained at the station."

"Just let us know," Maisy sobbed out.

Eli leaned forward and hugged her and touched his dad's shoulder. Then he left to tell everyone at the ranch. After he got that done he'd call Andie, make sure she was okay with the girls.

He pulled up to the ranch and parked. He stared at the large spread he and Caleb had worked so hard for together. He sighed as he got out of his truck and headed to the barn, he wasn't ready for any of this to be real but he had to accept it.

The few men turned toward him as he walked in.

"Hey, Boss, where's Caleb? Haven't seen him all morning," one of them called out.

"Well, that's where I've been. He and Candice were robbed and killed last night, the police don't know what all happened yet, we just have to wait and see if they figure it out," Eli explained trying not to be angry or upset at the moment.

All five of the guys stood there just staring at him. Some wide eyed, others frowning, one staring blankly.

"Once we figure out when Candice's family will be here we'll make arrangements for their funerals and everything, if you'll excuse me I need a few minutes." Eli made his way past the men and headed for his small office in the barn.

He slammed the door shut as soon as he entered it. He found the first thing he could, a wooden chair, and slammed it against the wall making it shatter as he let out a loud scream.

He was never going to see his brother again, twenty-nine

years of brotherhood wiped away because of some ass hat who couldn't make an honest living. He sank down to the floor, his back pressed against the wooden door. He pulled his hat from his head and threw it across the room, slammed his fist against the floor a couple times before he hung his head in his hands.

It wasn't fair, Caleb was only thirty-two, Candice twenty-five, they had so much more to live for, could have had so many more kids. Poor Lily would grow up not knowing who her parents really were or what they were like and how much they loved her.

He pulled out his phone once his anger calmed some, he went to his messages, he was glad after he had put his number in Andie's phone he had shot himself a text from her phone. He slid his thumb over the message to the right and it began to ring.

"Hello?" Her voice sounded so empty, he knew exactly how she felt. Although he wasn't taking care of two kids under the age of one.

"Andie, its Eli," he began.

"Well, I'd hope so, I mean your name popped up when you called," she said in a monotone voice.

"Right. Hey, did you get ahold of Candice's family?"

"I told you I'd handle it, so yeah, I handled it."

"How's Lily?" he tried to ignore the little bit of ice in her tone now.

"She's fine, sleeping finally."

"And what about you?"

"What about me?"

"Are you oaky?"

"Yup."

This conversation was going great. "Lucy?"

"Sleeping also. Look is there anything else you need me to do? I really don't want to be on here right now."

She was probably right, they both had been through hell

already and things were only going to get worse. "Do you need me to come get Lil?"

"No, she's finally asleep, after her being up all night I'd rather let her sleep." No life was coming into Andie's voice at all. Well, what do you expect, idiot? She just lost her best friend which, according to Caleb, was all the poor girl had besides Lucy.

"Do you need anything else?" he asked softly.

"No, do you?"

Hell, he needed a lot of things, a stiff drink, life to go back to the way it was. "Just to make sure you're okay and don't need anything."

"I'm fine, Eli." He heard her let out a deep breath.

"What about needing someone to watch the kids while you open the bakery?"

"I'm not opening today."

Man, talk about an unfriendly tone. "All right. Well, if you need anything don't be afraid to call me, I'll help."

She let out another sigh. "I'm fine, Eli. You take the time you need and be with your family, they need you, I can handle Lily."

"Okay, but the offer still stands."

"Thanks."

"You're welcome. I'll keep you updated about everything, when will her parents be here?"

"Not sure, they said just as soon as they could."

"All right, talk to you later." The line went dead in his ear. Who was she kidding? Sure she had a chip on her shoulder toward all the men around here, but it had never been that bad before. They were all hurting right now and could all use some support. But for some stupid reason, which exists because of one asshole's mistake, she wouldn't accept any support. She would give the support to Lily though.

Lily. What was going to happen to her now?

Andie stared at the phone for a minute after the conversation with Elijah Cameron. She let out a deep breath, she didn't want him knowing how much everything was killing her. She felt so numb and stupid and didn't even want to get up off the couch she had curled herself up on once the kids fell asleep.

Why couldn't he just leave her alone and mourn his loss like she was and not think twice about her? She let out a deep breath, she knew she had been cold, but what did someone expect when her faith in the opposite sex had been shattered. Just get through this and then once everything was over she would never have to see him again.

She slowly sat up from the couch then checked on Lily and Lucy. She smiled, they were still sawing logs. She began to move the play and pack carefully through the living room back to her bedroom so she could jump in the shower and still have them within ear shot in case something happened.

She turned the water up almost as high as it would go, she still felt so cold, she wondered if that feeling would ever go away. She shivered as the memory of seeing her best friend lying on that metal table filled her brain. She shook her head and tried to shut it all out. She never wanted to identify another body as long as she lived. Once was more than enough.

She got into the hot water and she shivered again as it ran across her skin but she still felt so cold and empty. She hoped they found whoever did this to her best friend and her husband, the ass hat didn't deserve to live after causing this much pain and sorrow. But for now she had to be strong for those two little girls sleeping in her bedroom. Especially for Lily. She was going to need stability after she realizes her parents weren't coming back. This was going to be a long road.

Chapter 3

Andie stayed in the shower until all the hot water was gone and it still had no effect on her cold body. She got out, dried off, then went to get dressed.

She decided on a pair of gray sweatpants and an oversized gray t-shirt that had the logo of her bakery 'Andie's Sweets' with two cupcakes with pink frosting and multi colored sprinkles.

She headed back to the play and pack where Lucy let out a squeal as she pulled herself up and Lily rolled to her knees and crawled over to the same side.

"You both are getting so big," she said happily which rewarded her with two big smiles. "Are we in better moods now?" she scooped Lily up first then Lucy and made her way out to the kitchen.

She placed Lily in a high chair and then Lucy. She first gave Lucy her plain cheerios and Lily her strawberry flavored puffs. They sat there stuffing their little faces while she began to fix their bottles and their baby food.

Strawberry-banana for Lily and peaches for Lucy. She sat down in front of them and alternated between the two of them. They were giggling and smacking their hands against their high chair tables.

Andie smiled, if only to be a child during this, not to fully understand what was happening, to not feel the heart ache.

She just was finishing up their baby food when a knock sounded at her door. She gave the girls some more puffs and cheerios. "I'll be right back, sweeties, behave," she said and kissed both their heads and headed to the door. She opened it to see a couple standing there.

Both were older, a tad wrinkly, the woman was wearing glasses in front of a pair of blue eyes and she had blonde hair. The man had salted brown hair with brown eyes.

"Mr. and Mrs. Howell?"

Rose Howell stepped forward and hugged Andie tightly. "We got here as soon as we could, are you okay, how's Lily?"

Andie hugged the plump older woman. "I'm okay, Lily seems to be okay after I finally got her to sleep some, we're in the kitchen just finishing up breakfast." Andie pulled back from Rose Howell and led her and her husband, Bruce, toward the kitchen.

Lily and Lucy were babbling at each other as they were smacking their hands on their high chairs.

Andie let a small smile touch her lips as Rose strolled forward and kissed her granddaughter on the head.

"You look so much like your momma," she whispered.

Andie felt the knife stab her heart as she thought of Candice, she let out a shaky breath as Lucy squealed. Andie shook her head and went to her daughter and handed Lucy the bottle she had made her.

Lucy took it and began to drink. Andie then grabbed Lily's bottle, "Here, Mrs. Howell, she's probably ready for this too."

Mrs. Howell loosened the tray and unfastened Lily. When she tried to pick Lily up, she let out a gut-wrenching cry, making Andie whip around.

Rose stood there frozen. "What happened?"

Andie stepped forward and placed a tender hand on Rose's shoulder. "She's been in a mood since last night." Andie picked Lily up and she instantly curled her fingers into Andie's hair and clutched her t-shirt in the other hand.

Andie bounced her up and down slowly. "Shh, shh, little one, it's okay, Mamaw just wanted to feed you your bottle." She rubbed Lily's back soothingly as she slowly began to settle down. "Will you let Mamaw hold you while Aunt Andie cleans up?"

Lily turned those expressive amber eyes on Andie, they were still swimming with tears making them a gold color. She pushed her face against Andie's shoulder and rubbed against it.

Andie repositioned Lily and took the bottle from Rose, when Lily took the nipple, Andie managed to give Lily back to Rose.

Andie grabbed the tray and turned to see Bruce getting Lucy. "It's okay, Mr. Howell. I can get her."

"It's okay, you got to clean her tray too, and it's my pleasure to take her." Bruce smiled his fatherly smile, but his brown eyes didn't light up as they usually did. But did she really expect them to?

She grabbed Lucy's tray and began to clean them both. She shoved her hands into the water just as her phone began to ring. "Oh great."

Rose answered it, "Hello? No, she's elbow deep in bubbles and water, we just arrived, yeah we can do that, I'm sure Andie can bring us out there, okay, we'll see you then." Rose hung up the phone and continued to feed Lily.

"Who was that?" Andie asked, turning around to fasten the trays back to the chairs.

"Eli Cameron," Rose answered, Andie drop the trays on the floor. Rose looked at her. "Are you okay?"

"Yeah, fine, um," Andie cleared her throat. "What did he want?" She tried to act calm.

"He wants us to meet out at the ranch Caleb and he ran together, he's taking his parents there in a little bit so we can discuss everything. We haven't been there since they had just started the business and moved out there. Will you take us there, dear?"

Andie picked up the trays grimacing to herself. "Of course, Mrs. Howell." She placed the trays back on the chairs and said, "Just let me get the girls changed and we can head out, where do you plan to stay?"

"Probably a hotel," Rose replied.

"You can stay here if you want to, I can take the couch or set up a spot in the nursery," Andie offered as she took Lily and Lucy.

"Nonsense, you won't give up your bed to us, we'll make do with a hotel," Bruce objected.

"Okay, but the offer still stands if you change your minds." Andie headed to the nursery, she placed Lucy on her feet first then Lily on the floor. She gathered their diapers, wipes and new clothes. She sat on the floor and stripped Lucy of her dirty clothes from breakfast and then Lily of hers.

She changed Lily's diaper while Lucy tried to get her toes in her mouth. "Lucy, don't do that right now, that's icky," Andie scolded her a little and Lucy sat back up and stared at Andie.

She dressed Lily in a cute pink onesie that said princess and matching pink pants with little crowns along them. She snatched Lucy up and changed her as well then put her in a purple onesie with a white cat on the front and purple pants.

Andie sat back and took a breather for a minute, running her fingers through her hair. She picked Lily up, then Lucy and headed out to the living room. She sat Lucy down on the couch and grabbed the bags throwing them over her shoulder and scooped Lucy back up.

She turned around seeing Bruce and Rose standing there. "What's the matter?" she asked, worry filling her.

"You handle both of them so well and quickly," Rose began.

"I've been having them both at least twice a week for six months now, I always take Lily when they have their date night," she paused and took in a sharp breath. "Are you guys ready to go?" she asked as she placed Lily in her carrier then Lucy in hers.

She grabbed the carriers as Bruce and Rose nodded and she headed out to the car. She put Lily's carrier in its base, then Lucy's and got in the driver's seat. Rose got in the passenger seat and Bruce got in the back beside Lily.

Andie took a deep breath as she started the car and made their way to the Cameron spread.

It wouldn't be her first time there but her first time without Candice there. Why them? She let out a shaky breath.

Andie's eyes darted around as she made her way along the long driveway. She took in the three huge white metal barns with green roofs. The two pastures, one full of cows, some reddish-brown and some black, the other with about ten horses of assorted colors.

The house was a beautiful log home. Candice had mentioned it was four thousand square feet. The main house was two stories and had a full finished basement. The outside of the second story had wood exterior with windows all around and the ground level had an exterior of dark stone with as many windows, the house was nestled in front of a mountain.

The back patio couldn't be seen from the front and had columns that supported the second story balcony.

The Camerons had done well for themselves, there were four bedrooms on the first floor and two down in the basement which had basically been Eli's domain.

She finally came to a stop beside Eli's gray truck. "I can come back when you guys are done," Andie offered.

Bruce was already getting Lucy out of her car seat. "Nonsense, you and Candice were friends for years, this involves you too, come on." He grabbed the bags and headed to the door as Andie got out to get Lily and the other bag.

Bruce apparently didn't want to upset Lily like Rose had earlier that morning. She walked up the steps as Rose knocked on the door. Andie didn't want to be here, she was no longer welcome now that Candice was gone.

Lucy let out a little cry and reached for Andie when Eli answered the door with a frown on his face.

Andie took Lucy as she adjusted Lily on to her other hip.

Eli looked past Mr. and Mrs. Howell and his gaze landed on the petite woman holding both girls again. She looked worse than last night, although her hair wasn't a jumbled mess.

He felt his frown soften as he met her tired, stress filled gray eyes. "Do you want me to take Lily?" he asked as he stepped aside and let Bruce and Rose walk in. What kind of grandparents didn't take their granddaughter, he thought?

"It's okay, I can handle it." Her tone wasn't as icy but still had a nip to it.

"Oh come on, Andie, I can help. I have better manners than that." He plucked his niece out of her arm and headed into the house as Andie followed after him.

He heard her shut the door behind herself and all hell

seemed to break loose. Lily let out a loud wail and squirmed in his arms, pushing against his chest.

He tried to adjust her. "Come on, Lily pad, what's the matter? Nana and Pop Pop are here. Do you want to see them?" It just set her off into a louder tizzy and she reached out for Andie.

"What did you do to my niece?" he demanded whirling around to the tiny woman standing behind him.

She frowned, placed her free hand on her hip and glared at him. "I didn't do anything to her."

"She's never been like this with me until you had her last night and today." He glared back at her.

He saw her gray eyes flash into hard steel. "She knows something is wrong, Eli, she feels all the tension from everyone. Just let me have her."

"So what are you saying, you're not tense, not upset about what's happened?" he glared harder at Andie. He didn't know what was setting him off beside the fact he was still so angry about his brother and sister-in-law and now his niece was having a fit in his arms. He saw her eyes break and change to a soft gray.

"No, that's... that's not... never mind." She turned to storm out of the house.

"What on earth is going on?" Maisy demanded rushing out of the living room.

"Nothing, Mom. Andie was just leaving." He adjusted Lily again who cried even louder and reached for Andie again.

"Why is she leaving? This involves her too," Maisy demanded frowning at him.

"She's apparently not upset about Caleb and Candice and doesn't put off tension upsetting Lily." He glared harder as Andie swung back around and glared back at him.

"I never said that, you said it. Look, you can't discuss anything with an upset baby crying, let me take her to her room. She didn't sleep well last night, let me see if I can get her to nap."

Eli practically growled at the suggestion.

Maisy took Lily from Eli and handed her to Andie. Lily immediately stopped crying and rubbed her face against Andie's shoulder.

"Mom…" he began.

"Elijah, just stop, we have enough going on!" Maisy squeezed Andie's shoulder, and said, "You can take her to her room, sweetie."

"Yes, ma'am." Andie headed down the hallway and turned into Lily's nursery.

"Mom…"

"Elijah, enough!" Maisy yelled.

He clamped his mouth shut quickly.

He called Detective Murphy, after his melt down, to find out when the mortuary could pick up Caleb and Candice. Two days. They had two days to figure everything out.

Andie couldn't believe the nerve of Eli. He was nothing like Caleb, Eli always let his temper get the best of him.

When she walked into Lily's nursery, she put Lucy on the floor with a few toys to keep her busy. She then stood by Lily's crib and rocked and soothed Lily until she fell asleep in her arms, then laid Lily down in her crib.

She sat on the floor by Lucy who played on the floor contently. "What are you doing, baby girl?" she asked as Lucy crawled up to her and pulled herself up. "You're getting so big," Andie told her.

Lucy laid her head on her shoulder and let out a yawn. Andie pulled her into her arms, "I know, sweetie, our schedule got a little messed up, are you ready for a nap too?"

Lucy rubbed her eyes with a tiny fist and yawned a little.

Andie cuddled Lucy and began to rock her back and forth slowly. Her pretty gray eyes slowly shut as she fell asleep also.

Andie managed to lay her down in the crib without waking her up. She covered her with another blanket. She turned the baby monitor on and went to get the other half from Candice and Caleb's room.

The door was shut, she laid her hand on the silver knob and slowly turned it. She walked into the peacock blue room and walked over to the dark dresser and grabbed the monitor.

Her eyes caught the two photos in a double frame on the dresser. She slowly picked it up, backed up to the end of the dark wooden sleigh bed frame and sat on the floor.

One picture was of the day she gave birth to Lucy and the other was the day Candice gave birth to Lily.

Tears filled her vision. She'd been so alone most of her life and only Candice had been there on the most important day of her life.

The tears fell rapidly down her cheeks as her finger traced the two pictures. And Eli thought she didn't care. Candice was the only family, besides Lucy, she had in the world and it was killing her.

She pulled the picture frame to her chest and sobbed uncontrollably. Her eyes slowly drifted shut as she continued to cry even in her sleep.

The parents and Eli managed to figure out what suit and dress Caleb and Candice would wear. The kind of caskets they'd have.

Eli went to get a drink and as he moved down the hallway to go to the kitchen at the back of the house he heard crying.

He frowned as he got closer to the nursery and it seemed to get louder.

Andie left them alone? He pushed the door open but Lily and Lucy were sound asleep. He pulled the door shut and headed farther down the hall when he noticed the master bedroom's door was cracked open. He heard the crying getting louder.

He pushed the door open and he heard the sobs and mumbling, "I can't look, don't make me, I can't do it."

He rushed into the room, his boots soundless on the plush gray carpet. He spotted Andie on the floor at the foot of the bed holding a picture close to her chest, tears were falling down her tan cheeks, repeating the words, 'no, I can't' over and over.

Eli flew over to her and knelt in front of her. "Andie, hey it's okay," he whispered to her.

She pulled away and continued to cry, he laid a hand on her shoulder, which made her jump and her eyes snapped open. She dropped the frame she was holding to the floor.

She quickly wiped her eyes and cheeks, she stood up stumbling a little, she grabbed the monitor and practically ran from the room.

He watched her leave, then he looked at his hand, she felt so cold through her t-shirt. She cared, she was just as upset.

God, you're an idiot, it's not even been twelve hours since she had to identify them, she's breaking inside, he scolded himself. He picked up the frame. Candice was all Andie had in the world. Caleb had told him a little about her bouncing from foster home to foster home until she was old enough to take care of herself.

She'd managed to stay in the same school district so she never lost Candice until she had moved here, found Caleb and married him.

Then Andie moved here a few months after the wedding, pregnant. She was braver than he gave her credit for, she was holding herself together because she never let anyone but Candice see her at her worse.

He set the picture back on the dresser as he took his hat off and raked a hand through his hair. He needed to apologize.

He went to find her but couldn't. He got his drink and went back to the living room to finish the talk he and the two sets of parents were having.

Andie escaped to the balcony deck. She shivered and wrapped her arms around herself tightly. How had she messed up and let him see her actually lose it?

She couldn't let it happen again. She would survive this by herself. No matter what.

She stood there losing track of time, she had no idea how long she had been out there when one of the girls began to stir. She went back in to check on them. Lucy was standing up in the crib and Andie picked her up, changed her diaper and let her play on the floor while Lily still slept.

After a little while Lily woke up, Andie changed her and she let the little girls play together.

Maisy came in and sat in the rocker.

"Mrs. Cameron," Andie greeted.

"Please, dear, Maisy is fine. Are you okay with Lil staying with you until we get everything situated?"

"Shouldn't you be asking Eli if he's okay with it? He sure does hate me," she mumbled as she watched Lily and Lucy play together.

"I don't care what Eli says, he'll mind his mother," Maisy said with a smile. "I feel Lily is better off with you right now, you're calmer than the rest of us, which isn't a bad thing, and she'd have Lucy to keep her company," Maisy explained softly.

Andie met her green eyes, they had so many feelings in

them, fear, sadness, anger, and a little bit of compassion. Andie looked back at the girls and said, "If that's what you want, Mrs. Cameron."

"At least until after the funerals and their wills are read."

"Yes ma'am."

"You can take whatever you need for Lily, if you need any help don't be afraid to call us."

Lily got on her knees and crawled to Andie, sat down in front of her reaching her hands up to Andie.

Andie slowly picked her up and she latched a hand into Andie's hair.

"She really does like you," Maisy whispered.

"And I love her as if she was my own." Andie stood up to start getting a few more of Lily's clothes. "When is the funeral?"

"Two days."

Andie found a little black frilly dress. "Will this be okay for it?" she turned holding up the dress to Maisy.

"I think it'll do. I better get back to the others," Maisy said as she left the room .

Andie nodded her head. She put Lily back on the floor with Lucy and quickly headed to the living room to get the diaper bag. She froze when she heard Eli's angry voice.

"I don't get why we should let her have Lily until after the funerals, it's stupid, she's running her own business, and already has a kid to take care of."

He really hated her.

Rose spoke next. "Where else should Lily go? She'll have a little companion in Lucy, Bruce and I are staying in a hotel, she won't be happy there, and you are busy with this huge ranch, Todd and Maisy and we are planning for two funerals, it makes sense."

Andie closed her eyes briefly and hurried into the room, grabbed the diaper bag and went back to the nursery. She grabbed Lucy and Lily and a blanket then left the house shutting the door a little more forcefully than she should have.

If he wanted to act so cold to her when she did nothing but love his niece then she could be just as cold, if not colder. He was a man after all and if they weren't old enough to be her father she wanted nothing to do with them. If she needed anything else for Lily she would just get it herself.

Eli flinched when he heard the house door slam. He really needed an attitude adjustment and fast.

Chapter 4

Andie was almost going stir crazy, she still hadn't opened the bakery and it felt so odd to not be in her comfort zone of baking and frosting her delicious cupcakes. But she knew she needed the time. She still wasn't sleeping, all she saw when she closed her eyes were Caleb and Candice laying on those metal tables, covered with those white sheets.

She was still keeping everything under control with the babies and Lily was working back into her normal schedule but she just couldn't sleep. She must be one hell of a pansy. Maybe after today she could put it all behind her.

She had already dressed in her half sleeved, slightly tight black dress. It came down to her knees and there was nothing special about it, just a plain black dress. She also found a pair of flat black dress shoes, since she'd never worn heels a day in her twenty-five years.

She dressed Lily in her frilly black dress and placed her back on the floor then caught Lucy before she crawled away. She dressed Lucy in her black onesie and matching skirt and sat her on the couch, then she picked up Lily and the bags. She turned to Lucy, helping her stand then scooped her up as well.

Andie took a deep breath as she headed for the door. She struggled to open it but finally managed and pulled it shut with her foot. She shivered as she stepped outside even though it was almost seventy degrees, what was wrong with her?

She shook her head, walked to the car and stood Lucy on the concrete driveway while she opened the car door. She put Lucy on the seat, placed Lily in her car seat, and fastened her in. Leaving the bags on the floor of the back seat she picked Lucy up, put her in her car seat and fastened her in. She grabbed her keys from the diaper bag, got in the driver's seat, started the car and headed to the church. Rose and Bruce were getting a ride from Todd and Maisy.

There was going to be a short viewing before the funeral. She hadn't been asked to speak and that was fine with her. She didn't know what to really say. She was just so… empty and sad but she pushed through for Lily and Lucy.

After the funeral and burial they were going to hear Caleb and Candice's will. Then they would make the necessary arrangements for Lily.

Andie smiled a little as she heard the two babies gabble back and forth. Like they were having their own little conversation.

She pulled into the parking lot of the small white church letting out a deep breath. She got out of the car leaving the windows down, she got Lucy out then went around to the other side to get the bags and Lily. She swung the bags over her neck and placed Lucy on the seat. She got Lily out, placed her on her hip, then put Lucy on her other hip. She adjusted both girls and struggled to close the door.

Eli was out front of the church talking to a couple of his employees and friends when his gaze landed on the small spitfire. "Excuse me guys, I'll be right back," he took off heading over to Andie.

He got a little closer and she managed to close the car door. As she turned to head to the church they both froze.

They hadn't spoken or seen each other since his outburst at the house. She looked worse than she had that day. But seeing her show off those tan legs of hers again sent him reeling. She was so beautiful.

Wait, what? Where the hell did that come from? he mentally kicked his own ass, he was supposed to be grieving two family members, not thinking his sister-in-law's best friend was beautiful. He shook himself out of the thought and continued to walk over to her.

It didn't even look like she breathed once as he strolled over to her. "Hey, Andie, let me help?" He held out his hands and was surprised when Lucy reached her little arms out and latched onto his black suit sleeves. He placed his huge hands around Lucy and pulled her from Andie.

Her gaze narrowed a little and they were still a steely color instead of the soft, warm gray Lucy's had. He needed to apologize, which he was never good at. She began to walk to the church and he followed right behind her, his gaze raked over her a little more.

Stop it you stupid lug head! he scolded himself as they entered the overcrowded church. He stepped closer to her and laid a hand against the small of her back.

Her head snapped up and she shot a gun metal glare at him but he ignored it and ushered her into the sanctuary and found her a pew to sit at. He sat down beside her but kept a respectable distance.

She unloaded the bags from her shoulder and adjusted Lily. A smile played on both of the baby's lips as Lucy and Lily grabbed each other's hands and babbled nonsense to each other.

Eli could see the girls were becoming even closer. He glanced at Andie, she had turned her head away from him and was staring straight ahead, "I can take Lily for a minute if you want to say your goodbyes," he offered softly.

He watched a wave of sadness wash across Andie's face but it was hard in the next instant as she shook her head. He looked at her a moment longer, she was really being affected but she wouldn't let anyone know it. He just hoped she wouldn't break down and totally lose it. Although she had a right to do so.

Maybe once she didn't have to care for both girls she'd be better. "Andie, I'm–"

"Eli, we need you for a minute," his father called out.

Eli looked to his dad. "Okay." He looked back to Andie. "Do you want me to try to take Lily?"

All she did was shrug her shoulders in response. He put Lucy in her lap and placed his hands around Lily, the back of his hand inadvertently brushed against one of her breasts.

He felt her tense up and pull back quickly. He didn't say anything as he moved Lily into his arms to get a better hold of her and she let out a loud cry, making many of the guests turn to look.

Andie looked at Eli and Lily and Lily reached out for her.

Eli heard the many murmurs of, "Who brings babies to a funeral?" and "Can't she control those kids?" He turned to glare at the people who turned away quickly.

He placed Lily beside her, and said, "I'll be back to help in a minute." He headed over to his dad.

"I don't need help." He heard her murmur as Lily began to settle down.

He shook his head and rolled his eyes. Stubborn woman. He headed over to his dad, "What's up?"

"She wasn't too thrilled about having you over there, figured I'd give you an excuse to get away."

Eli frowned at Todd. "What the heck? I was just getting ready to apologize."

"Really?" His dad sounded shocked. He glanced to Andie who was carefully watching both girls. "I think it's going to take more than an apology with her."

"I don't know, she let me help her inside with Lucy, I don't want an enemy with her." Eli glanced back just as Lucy almost fell off the pew but Andie reacted fast and wrapped her arm around her and pulled Lucy into her while keeping hold of Lily.

She made Lucy sit down beside her making Lucy let out an upset squeal.

Eli let out a sigh. "I'm going to see if I can help her some more." He started to walk over but Todd grabbed him by the shoulder. Eli turned to look at his dad and asked, "What?"

"Don't, Eli. We don't need another scene like we had at the house."

He let out a sigh as he stared at Andie. "Fine." He gave in.

Andie's heart was pounding from the way Lucy had latched onto Eli, the way his hand had felt on her back, and then Lucy almost falling off the pew.

Maybe she should have just stayed home. It was obvious the people there thought she shouldn't be here.

She was sitting alone in the back. She got shunned a lot when she was out but people sure didn't have a problem eating her sweets and other foods she baked.

The service was just getting started and Lily began to get a little cranky. Lily let out a squeal as Eli got up to speak, making quite a few people turn to look at her, Lily, and Lucy. She picked up the bags and babies then began to walk out. Yeah. Terrible idea. She bit back the tears as she struggled with the door to exit the sanctuary.

Eli looked up when he heard his niece and stopped speaking as people turned to look at Andie. He couldn't just watch as she pulled open the door and left with the babies. He stopped and took a step to go after her when he heard a throat clear and looked at his dad. Eli took a deep breath and continued the speech he had prepared.

As soon as he was done, he stepped down and instead of taking his seat by his parents he exited the sanctuary. He finally found Andie sitting outside with a blanket spread on the grass under a huge oak tree.

She was playing with both girls, and he observed how she didn't show Lily any less attention than she did Lucy. The babies were laughing as she tickled their feet and bellies.

He smiled as he headed over. "You didn't have to leave, you know."

She looked up at him, her gray eyes were soft this time, she shrugged her shoulders. "It's okay."

He sat down next to her at an angle, stretching his long legs out behind her and leaned back onto one of his hands. "No, it's not, Andie, she was your best friend."

"Some seem to have forgotten that." She shot a glance at him as a small breeze blew her hair across her cheek.

He reached out and tucked it behind her ear, he heard the sharp breath she inhaled. "I'm sorry about the other day," he whispered.

She shrugged her shoulders. "It's fine, I get it. It's unacceptable here to be a single mom to one baby, let alone try to take care of two. I'm used to it by now."

"I don't feel that way, things happen that can't be controlled sometimes," he offered.

"It could have been, if I hadn't been so stupid," she whispered, as Lucy crawled over to Eli and pulled herself up on him.

"Hey, cutie, not scared of me today, huh?" He put a hand against her back as she bounced up and down a little and gurgled.

Lily sat up slowly and latched on to Andie's dress and hair and pulled herself up also.

Eli watched wide-eyed, "That's new."

Andie pulled out her phone and typed something quickly then hugged Lily. "Such a great job, sweetie, you're getting so big, you don't want to be outdone by Lucy do you?" she praised. She glanced at Eli and took Lucy. "You better get back inside before someone sees that you're out here with me, you don't want that to happen."

Eli let out a sigh. "You could come back in, I'll help."

She shook her head. "No, it's fine."

He laid a hand on her shoulder. "Are you coming to the cemetery?"

"I don't know. I don't know if I'll be at the reading of their will either, Rose and Bruce can let me know what the plan is and I'll comply."

"I want you to come, you will have whatever you want of Candice's things, her parents agreed with me, so at least show up there?"

She let out a sigh. "Okay, thanks, Eli."

He rubbed her shoulder a little, she still felt cold to him but he didn't know what to do to help her.

He got up and headed back inside. He returned just in time for the end of the service.

Andie sat there with Lily and Lucy and watched as Eli, Todd, Bruce, and a couple of other men loaded up the first casket. She fought the tears as they headed back in and brought out the second casket.

The girls crawled into her lap and she pushed the tears away as they clung to her. What if she let Eli in to help a little right now? Could she have mourned the loss of her friend?

No, terrible idea, she was already craving his scent of dark chocolate, hay, and leather soap. She shivered at the thought. And when he touched her he made her feel warm again. She also knew she could lose herself in those strange eyes of his, that would change color depending on his mood. When he was being sweet like he just had been they were a soft golden color instead of the coppery tint when he was upset or confused.

How did she get to be so perspective over that man? It wasn't like anything could ever happen because she wouldn't allow it. She would wait until after the will reading, once Lily was no longer in her care before she would allow herself to lose it and mourn her best friend. Lucy wasn't as tense as Lily was because Lily did know something was wrong, she just didn't know what.

She would be okay until then, hell, she didn't even think she wanted anything of Candice's, all she wanted was her best friend back. Maybe something would bring peace to her. Doubtful. So doubtful.

Chapter 5

Andie pulled up to Eli's home, but no one was there yet. She put the car in park, and shook her head as she remembered she needed to change the oil and spark plugs and wires.

She shut the car off, grabbed a sticky note and pen then began to make a list of things she needed to do. She definitely needed oil, a filter, spark plugs, and wires before she went home today.

The gutters needed to be cleaned out at her house, the leaky faucet needed to be replaced at the bakery, her lawn needed to be mowed along with the bakery's. A few of the tables at the bakery needed to be tightened to their bases, the toilet needed a new valve inside the tank.

She had to open up tomorrow, she needed to bake, it would relax her. She began to make a list of everything she would bake once the will was read and she could go home.

She glanced up and realized people were showing up finally. She got out of the car, grabbed the diaper bags then Lucy. She unhooked Lily's car seat, set it down next to the car, removed the base from the car and held it in her free hand then picked Lily up in the carrier. She headed up to the house, she sat Lily down and opened the door.

She shut the door with her foot juggling everything as she did. No one offered to help her, not that she expected it, nor did she expect the sexy, well dressed, cowboy to come sauntering over to her.

"Here, Andie, let me take Lucy." Eli didn't give her a chance to refuse.

He pulled Lucy from her arm but she was a little grateful. She took Lily out of the carrier and moved the carrier and base out of the way. "So, when are we doing the will?" She looked up into Eli's eyes and she wished she wouldn't have. They were so yellow at the moment, they sent a shiver down her spine.

"After we eat," Eli answered putting his hand on the small of her back, a little firmer than he had at the church. The warmth spread across her body, she wanted to lean closer to him but she knew she couldn't. His scent was already wafting through her nose.

He led her to the kitchen, where he actually got food for her, grabbed two extra plates and took her out on the balcony deck that was empty.

He placed the food on one of the chairs as she sat in the other one. "Do you have that blanket still?"

She began to dig in one of the bags and pulled it out.

He took it from her and managed to spread it out, he sat Lucy down on it and grabbed the two empty plates. "Snacks for the kids?" his deep voice rumbled.

Andie sat Lily down on the blanket then pulled out the cheerios and puffs. "Lucy likes the cheerios only, and I'm sure you know Lily likes the strawberry puffs."

He smiled at her and took the plastic baggies. He poured some cheerios for Lucy and the puffs for Lily.

Andie smiled but then it faded when she realized she was

going to lose Lily after today. She'd never have to watch her again. Eli would take care of everything from now on.

Lucy and Lily would more than likely lose each other until they began school.

She felt a nudge against her shoulder and she looked up to see Eli handing her the plate with food. She took it but only nibbled at it.

"Come on, Andie, you've got to eat," he encouraged with a stern tone.

How did he do that? she wondered. *And why did it make her feel almost tingly?* Even though she didn't agree with him. She wasn't hungry, hadn't been since she had run from the cold room and gotten sick. She only nibbled at the food as her eyes watched Lucy and Lily carefully.

Eli sat on the deck floor beside the girls as they ate. His gaze would flick to Andie every now and then. She still hadn't eaten much.

He heard the door slide open behind him, he looked back to see his dad standing there.

"We were wondering where you ran off to, everyone's left for the most part, the lawyer is ready."

"Okay, let us get the girls cleaned up and we'll be in in a minute." He checked that the girls were finished with their snacks and scooped Lucy up while Andie took Lily.

Hopefully one day he'd be able to hold his niece again. He leaned down to get the blanket, throwing it over his shoulder and made his way to the door.

As they walked in they threw the plates away and he laid his hand against her back firmer than he had the last two times, she was warming up to him slowly and he was pushing to find out how much warmer could he get her. He moved her toward the den where they would be having the meeting.

He had brought in an oval table that had a chair at the head of the table for the lawyer, four on the one side for his and Candice's parents and two on the other side for Andie and himself. He pulled one of the chairs back and gestured for Andie to sit, once she did he pushed her back up to the table. He sat down beside her.

Andie kept her gaze down at the table, looking at all the rings the wood had designed all by itself. She felt the eyes of Rose, Bruce, Maisy, and Todd all on her. Her heart was pounding, she didn't have the right to be here.

Lily all of a sudden squealed and pushed her fingers into Andie's mouth. Andie pulled them away and turned her toward the table and went to reach for one of her toys out of the diaper bag.

She handed the toy to Lily as the lawyer cleared his throat. Andie glanced up, the man looked so young but had a full head of pure white hair, he had pretty deep-blue eyes and was in a snazzy gray suit.

"All right, are we ready to begin?" he asked.

Everyone but Andie answered.

"Okay, well they wanted their possessions divided between the family, Mr. and Mrs. Cameron and Elijah Joseph Cameron, you can divide Caleb's things amongst you as you see fit, Mr. and Mrs. Howell you get all of Candice's personal possessions, I've been informed that Andrea Nicole Malone gets to decide what she wants of Candice's things, and everyone agrees to that, correct?" His sharp eyes darted around to look at everyone who all nodded their heads in agreement.

Andie turned her eyes back to the little girl on her lap who was now chewing on the toy. This was it, she rubbed her thumb in a circular motion against Lily's chunky thigh. She could already feel her heart breaking.

"Now, the most important part, everyone in this room has a connection to Lillian Nicole Cameron, an uncle, grandparents, a friend of the mother who watched her quite a bit. I understand she has been with Andrea Nicole Malone for the past few days due to the circumstances and trying to figure everything out." He paused as his eyes flew over the will. "And the arrangement will remain as is. Candice and Caleb talked to me long and hard about this, they thought it through the minute they discovered they were going to have a baby. In the event something should happen to them at the same time, the custody of Lillian Nicole Cameron would go to Andrea Nicole Malone, the child's Godmother."

Andie's head snapped up to look at the lawyer, just as Eli jerked out of the chair so hard and fast it sent the chair flying behind him, creating a hole in the drywall.

"How the fuck is that even possible? She's not even blood to Lily!" he yelled so loud it almost shook the house.

Andie sat there for a moment in shock until Lucy began to scream and cry, she stood up. "Eli, give me Lucy, now." Her voice was pure ice. How dare the man scare her daughter. She was actually surprised he kept ahold of Lucy during his dramatic scene.

He seemed to ignore her. "She's already a single mom with a ten-month old, how the hell is she supposed to take care of an eight-month old also?" Eli demanded, slamming his fist down on the table. "Lily should be with family, I'm at least her uncle."

That did it for Andie, she grabbed the diaper bags and pulled Lucy from him. "Maybe they knew you would be too hot-headed to take care of a child." Andie glared at him as he looked at her, his eyes flaming with anger.

Andie tried to soothe Lucy when Lily suddenly began to cry.

"You can't take care of two kids that close in age by yourself," he yelled at her.

"Elijah!" Maisy tried to interject.

"At least I won't send things flying into a wall scaring the kids I will be taking care of. And I will do it by myself, and no hot-headed, arrogant jerk will tell me otherwise! You don't know me well enough to tell me what I can and can't do or how determined I can and will be." She turned from the table and began to leave. "The only thing I want of Candice's is the framed photos of us on the days we gave birth to our daughters, just mail it to me, ass hat."

Andie's blood was boiling, how dare that man try to tell her what she could and couldn't do. She would never let another man bring her down like that, it wasn't like she was thrilled to have two babies in her care but by God she would uphold her best friend and her husband's request.

She bounced both girls trying to calm them down. And to think she was just starting to trust Elijah Cameron after his stupid apology, which meant absolutely nothing, and when he told her he didn't feel the same as others did around there.

Never trust a man. She rushed to the living room, she sat a crying Lucy by her feet and managed to get Lily calm enough to buckle her in the carrier. She picked up Lucy trying to get her to calm down also. Then she picked up the carrier and turned around, freezing when she saw those russet eyes on her.

"Andie, you know this isn't fair to you."

"Oh well, it is what it is, and I'll do it. Candice and Caleb wanted this, and until you get your head out of your ass and your temper under control you won't be around my daughter or Lily. Lily's going through enough as it is." She stormed past Eli.

He stepped in front of her as she walked past him.

She glared at him. "Move out of my way."

"Let me help."

"No." She moved around him and continued down the hallway. She managed to grab the base for Lily's carrier and opened the door shutting it in his face as he followed her down the hallway.

She hurried to her car she placed Lucy on the seat while she tried to get the base fastened back in the car. Lucy began to pull on her hair as she tried to get it fastened.

Tears threatened her but she pushed them away. No man would ever tell her what to do again.

Eli rushed out the door after Andie, he saw her struggling in the car and heard her telling Lucy to stop. He pulled Andie out of the car along with Lucy, finished fastening the base into the car and then put Lily's carrier in it.

He took Lucy from Andie and placed her in her seat, surprised she didn't cry being in his arms after his stupid outburst.

"Eli, just stop, I can do it." She followed him around the car pulling out her keys. He took those from her as well and started the car, turned on the air, waited for the air to cool, and put the windows up.

He got out shutting the door and pulled Andie up against him then spun them so her back was pressed against the car. "The minute I find out you are struggling or can't take care of both of them I swear I will get custody of Lily, I will go along with this for now." He watched her soft gray eyes harden to pure steel.

"Bring it on, Eli, I'm not afraid of you. I love Lily as much as you do and I refuse to cower before you. I will raise her the way Candice and Caleb would have, even if I can't buy the fanciest things in the world for her, she will never go without."

As they stood there, their bodies pressed together something stirred inside Eli. He wanted her. She was so strong willed, and wasn't afraid of him like most were, she stood her ground and glared back at him and even called him an ass hat. Yeah, he was being one that was for sure.

He couldn't have thoughts like this, he had to get custody of his niece, Andie was nothing to Lily and Lily needed to be with family.

"Now, let me go." Andie's voice was pure coldness on his ears, just like her body was against his.

He searched her eyes and saw nothing but cold, hard, determination. He pushed himself away from and her and she wasted no time.

She turned away from him, got into her car, turned it around and began to leave.

He stared after the car wanting to yell, throw something, or punch something. She had no claim to Lily and he would prove she was unfit. No matter what it took.

Andie rushed away from the Cameron property, never in a million years did she think Candice and Caleb would make her Lily's Godmother. Sure she'd made Candice Lucy's Godmother but that had made perfect sense, Andie had no one else. They could have chosen Eli as Lily's Godfather and custody holder but why didn't they?

She drove trying to keep her body from shaking from the adrenaline swimming through her veins after the fight with Eli, and the way he pushed his body against hers, she shivered a little. There was just something about the man that awoke so many feelings inside of her. Fear. Hate. Need. But she would give in to none of it.

Once he calmed down she would let him be around Lily but he would never get close to her or Lucy and that was final.

She glanced at her steering wheel with the note of things she needed done. She let out a sigh, they still needed done, even with having two babies to take care of.

She stopped at the auto store and hardware store, where she got some very distasteful looks but it didn't stop her.

Once home she fed the girls, gave them their baths then put them in their jammies. She would take nothing from Candice and Caleb's home, anything she would need for Lily she would get on her own. She would never step foot inside that house again. As the girls played on the floor together in perfect harmony, Andie began to think about the things she would need.

Clothes were about the only things that weren't necessary. She had most of Lucy's old clothes and she could use what were in good shape for Lily until things settled down and she could go buy her some new ones.

She placed her order for a new crib, more toys that Lily loved, bottles, and anything else she could think of. She put her phone down on the couch.

Everything would be delivered the day after tomorrow, until then they would make do.

As the kids started to get tired, Andie picked them up and began to make her way over to the bakery. She needed something to keep her mind off of everything.

And to think Eli had been so sweet to her at the church and then he just flipped like a light switch. His attitude may have gotten him what he wanted in the past but this was one battle he wasn't going to win.

She got to the bakery and headed over to the little play area – which took up one corner of the room – with the wrap around gate and placed the girls on the padded floor. It was about four inches thick.

She watched Lily and Lucy lay down and start to fall asleep. She covered them each with a blanket, grabbed the video monitor and took it back with her to the kitchen and began to bake her goodies for the next day.

She couldn't stay closed forever, especially now that she had two babies to care for. She dove into her work glancing at the monitor to make sure the girls were okay.

"Elijah, all of that was uncalled for," Maisy scolded as she walked out on the front porch a half hour after Andie left. "What did all that really gain you?"

He shot a look at his mom and just shrugged his shoulders. "Why is she named guardian when she's not even blood?"

Maisy let out a sigh and sat on the wooden porch swing with him. "I think they were right in doing it, your temper is out of hand, Eli. I know we're all stressed but Andie is the only one who has kept it fully together for Lily's sake. Your father and I are too old to be running after a baby like Lily, so are Candice's parents. Caleb and Candice went with the one who is the best fit for Lily and won't lose her temper at the drop of a hat."

"She can't keep it together forever, she's eventually going to break."

"And wouldn't you rather be there for her, to help pick up the pieces, instead of trying to push her further to her breaking point?" Maisy demanded. "You were so sweet to her at the church, then poof you don't get what you want and you pushed her away, scared Lucy, and made a real ass out of yourself. Your father and I did not raise you to be like this. Once you open your eyes and realize Lily is better off with Andrea the less angry you will be. You can be sweet to her, it will not kill you, hell, maybe you two could even end up being together. I've seen the way you two have looked at each other the last couple of years she has been here."

Eli let out a snort. "Yeah, right, she doesn't need a man, she's said that over and over again, she doesn't need help."

"But that doesn't mean that's not what she wants. This town hasn't been too friendly to her, so maybe she doesn't need a man, but she does need friends. Candice is gone, Eli, just like Caleb but you still have something that Andrea doesn't, you still have family and friends. Andrea now has two little girls to provide for and no one is in her corner, it's not always going to be easy for her."

Eli looked at his mom, why did she always have to be right? How was he going to get Andie to trust him again after what he promised her he would do to her if he found out she couldn't take care of Lily? Not that he really thought that, he was just so angry that Caleb pushed him on the back burner. Now he had to figure out how to fix it.

Chapter 6

Andie was in her little shop with gray walls and pink table tops. She was rushing to get everyone what they wanted. Whenever she was in eye shot of the girls she would glance over at them to make sure they were okay.

When she didn't have them in her sight she would constantly look at the video monitor. And, of course, they were okay.

The crowd finally began to disperse and everything was gone as usual. As the last customer left she locked the door and began to clean up. She was back in the kitchen when she heard a knock.

She let out a sigh as she loaded up the dishwasher and headed back to the dining area.

She froze when she saw Eli outside the door.

He raised his hands up in a peaceful gesture and he looked calm. She frowned at him and folded her arms over her chest.

He said something but she couldn't really hear him. She just raised her eyebrows at him. She tried not to laugh as he hung his head for a minute. He pulled out his phone and seemed to type something.

Her phone pinged in her apron pocket. She frowned at him but slowly pulled her phone out and read the message from him.

I'm sorry, can I see Lil?

She looked up at him and slowly walked over to the door. She unlocked it and opened it but didn't let him in right away. "Are you going to keep your temper in check?"

"Yes, the minute I don't you can throw me out," he answered trying to win her over with a smile.

She rolled her eyes and stepped back letting him in. "They're over in the playpen," she said, then locked the door and headed back to clean the kitchen while Eli went to the playpen.

She watched the monitor for a minute and smiled at his interaction with Lily. He had climbed into the playpen and was tickling her, making her laugh.

Andie finished wiping the counters, oven, and sinks. She glanced at the monitor and saw Eli still playing with Lily and Lucy was off on the other side of the playpen playing by herself.

She slowly sank down to the floor and put her head in her hands. She rubbed her face with both hands and took a deep breath.

She stood up and heard a loud wail. She ran out to the playpen and saw Eli talking to Lucy. She pulled Lucy into her arms and began to bounce her up and down.

Eli looked at Andie as she pulled Lucy from him, she looked so tired. She had strands of hair falling around her face. He stood up taking Lily but she let out a cry too.

Andie took her also and tried to get her to calm down. "Sorry, Eli, it's time for them to eat."

"I could help," he offered and smiled at her.

She narrowed those gray eyes of hers at him. "What about the ranch?"

"Eh, the guys got it for now, I want to help."

She let out a sigh. "Fine." She turned away from him and headed toward the door.

He rushed past her feeling like he'd gained a victory as he opened the door for her. "Keys?"

"Left apron pocket," she answered. "If you take Lily I'll get them out."

Instead, he reached into her pocket, pulled them out and locked up. He followed her to the house next door. He unlocked her front door and pushed it open, letting her walk in first.

He followed her to the kitchen where she placed Lily in a highchair then Lucy. His gaze followed her as she strapped in one then the other, then went to the fridge and got four jars of baby food. She pulled two baby spoons from a drawer and came back over to them.

She pulled two chairs up in front of the highchairs and she seemed to collapse into one. He sat beside her and held out his hands to take the food so he could feed Lily. She handed them to him, their fingers brushed against each other and his eyes darted to hers. He felt the coldness in her fingertips but he didn't say anything.

She pulled her hand back quickly, and said, "Just half of each jar."

"Okay," he answered but found himself wanting to know how to make her feel better. He began to feed Lily and while he was darting his eyes between her and Andie, Lily managed to whack the spoon out of his hand. It went flying into Andie covering her cheek and some of her hair with the food that had been on it.

He had to fight not to laugh at the sight.

She turned to look at him, her eyebrows raised. He saw the paper towels on the counter behind her. He stood up quickly and grabbed them.

He came back to her, ripping a towel off and began to clean her face and hair, "I'm so sorry, Andie."

She looked at him. "What; did you throw that at me?" Her eyebrows raised even more.

He let out the laugh he was holding in as he wiped clean the baby food covered strands of brown hair, he'd never noticed the caramel highlights in her hair that seemed natural before, and answered, "No, I didn't. I just wasn't paying attention and Lily got a hold of the spoon."

She shook her head and rolled her eyes. "Well, thanks for cleaning me up," she said, and blushed, as she continued to feed Lucy.

He smirked and continued to feed Lily.

As they finished Eli glanced at Andie and asked, "How do you do this for both of them?"

She shrugged her shoulders and replied, "I just do it."

He shook his head. "Well, now what?"

"Usually I put them in their room and let them play, so I can shower and wash the day away," she answered simply.

"How do you keep an eye on them?"

"Video monitor, it also has sound but I am usually only in the shower for maybe ten minutes."

He looked her over as she went to get Lucy then Lily. He never knew all of that was possible. Apparently Candice and Caleb knew what they were doing. "Well, I'm here, I'll watch them for you. Why don't you soak in the tub for a little bit?" he suggested innocently.

She narrowed those beautiful gray eyes of hers at him before replying, "No, I'm good. I won't be long." She made her way down the hallway and went into a room.

As he walked in behind her he saw the one crib. "They both sleep in there?" he asked.

"It's not ideal, I'm working on getting another crib."

"Why don't you just take the one from the house?" he asked.

"Well, you're determined to take her from me, so is there any point in taking anything from there?"

He grimaced a little and softly said, "Andie."

"Nope, it's fine, I get it. If you take her, I'm not going to be able to stop you. I'll fight, but I can't stop it." Her voice turned icy.

She kissed Lucy and Lily, then headed out of the room after she got toys for them.

He sat down on the brown carpeted floor and watched the girls interact together. He hated himself for the last conversation he had with Andie. He thought maybe it had been forgotten since she let him be around Lily. He was wrong obviously.

This was going to be harder than he thought.

Andie made her way to her bedroom and got a change of clothes which was black sweatpants and a black tank top, a pair of pink panties, and pink bra.

She must be a fool to have let Eli into her home. Sure he had the right to see Lily and she didn't want to keep them apart, but just yesterday he had threatened to take Lily away from her. She was determined to make him see she could take care of both children, herself, and the bakery.

He had nothing on her nor would he get anything.

She headed to the bathroom and shut the door. She laid her clothes on the small black vanity top then started the shower.

Maybe she could take a few extra minutes? She stripped out of her work clothes and laid her phone by her clean clothes, then got into the shower. She let out a sigh as the water pounded against her skin.

She washed her body, her hair, and shaved. She stayed in a little bit longer until her thoughts began to drift to Candice and Caleb. She shut the water off and got out, dried, then got dressed.

She brushed her hair hastily and went to the girls' bedroom. She had to stop and just stare at what she was looking at, she leaned against the doorjamb. She couldn't fight the smile as she saw Lucy wearing Eli's hat while he was blowing raspberries on Lily's belly, but as soon as Lucy wanted attention he would blow raspberries on her cheeks and nibble them, making her squeal with laughter.

Wait, he wasn't supposed to be near her or Lucy after yesterday. But the sight was just too adorable. A six-foot-four man on his knees playing with two little girls like that was priceless.

For a fleeting moment she wondered what it would have been like to raise Lucy with her real father but that was just stupid childish nonsense.

It had been a fluke that she even got pregnant. She had been told she would never have kids and her boyfriend at the time was still using protection.

The day she found out she was pregnant began to replay in her mind, she had been a month late, and she'd been feeling so sick. While he was at work one day, she called off, went to the store and bought a test.

It hadn't even taken the full three minutes for the results. She had sat there on the couch with the test in her hand while she had called Candice in tears. Telling her how Daryl hadn't wanted kids.

Candice had tried to reassure her, but nothing helped.

That day she had found out how much Daryl didn't care. She'd still been sitting on the couch when he came home.

First, he was irate that she hadn't gone to work, then the fact she hadn't had supper ready, then he saw the test. That had been the first and last time he had hit her and actually tried to make her lose Lucy.

That was also her first trip to Whitehorse. When Caleb and Candice weren't living with Eli. She had stayed with them until the bruises healed, never leaving the house. She had gone back to North Dakota and shortly later Candice told her the news about getting married.

Andie decided then that she needed her best friend. She had been four months pregnant at Candice's wedding and no one knew. She was six months along by the time she managed to officially move to Whitehorse and Candice told her she was four months pregnant.

Andie let out a shaky breath as tears threatened to fall.

Eli looked up when he heard the sigh, his gaze landed on Andie. Tears were in her eyes, she looked as if she was so lost. He stood up quickly and walked up to her. "Andie, what's wrong?" he cupped her cheeks gently. "Andie?"

She jerked from his hands and moved back from him. "Nothing, it's just time for the girls' naps." She walked around him and began to change their diapers and then she laid them down on the opposite sides of the crib, they yawned and slowly began to fall asleep.

She turned away from the crib and picked up Eli's hat from the floor. She slowly handed it to him and began to leave the nursery.

Eli followed her, they got out to the living room and he

caught her arm and pulled her back toward him, he cupped her cheek gently, rubbing his thumb against her cheek, and softly asked, "What was really wrong back there, Andie?"

She shook her head but didn't move from him.

"Something happened back there, was it me?" he asked, worried he had upset her somehow.

She shook her head as she pulled her full bottom lip between her teeth and chewed on it.

He rubbed her arm gently as his other hand threaded through her damp brunette, caramel highlighted hair.

Her eyes slowly closed.

"Why don't you take a nap? I can watch the girls," he whispered, wishing she would let him hug her but he knew that would be pushing it.

She shook her head a little, "I have so much I have to do, I can't take a nap." She slowly stepped back from him.

He searched her mesmerizing gray eyes and moved closer to her again. "Like what?"

"Normal things that you would have people do for you," she whispered and went to step back from him again.

He pulled her back to him though and wrapped his arms around her, her head against his chest, then her arms slowly wrapped around his waist but loosely.

He stood there just holding her, the feel of her little, but very womanly, body felt so amazing against him. Why had it taken so long for him to realize he wanted to get to know her even better?

There was so much Caleb hadn't told him because he had shut down so many opportunities feeling it was useless information. He had been so focused on trying to get the ranch up and running, he wanted no distractions. And a female with an adorable child was not in the plan. Caleb hadn't felt the same way, the minute he had set his eyes on Candice he was lost.

He rubbed her back gently as he tilted his head down laying it against the top of her head. He took in a deep breath and the scent of roses, vanilla, and sugar sent goosebumps along his skin. She smelled so delicious and it seemed no matter how long she had been in that shower, she couldn't erase the smell of the bakery. He took in another deep breath.

All of a sudden her body tensed and she pulled away from him just as he felt her body start to warm.

She glanced up at him. "Maybe, you should go," she said and moved away. "Please, Eli, just go, I'll call you later this week and let you take Lily for a little bit." She moved further away when he moved closer to her.

He felt a little defeated but he really had screwed up. He went to walk past her slowly to go to the door.

He felt her smooth hand grasp his rough, callused one, he turned back to her a little.

"I really will call you later this week, Eli. I don't want to keep Lily from you, or Maisy and Todd, and I won't, you're her family," she whispered as she stared at the brown carpet.

He reached his other hand to her chin and tilted her head up slowly. "I know, it's okay, just don't forget you're not alone during all of this, you can count on certain people." He brushed her cheek with his thumb then headed out the door.

Andie followed behind him and shut and locked the door as he left. She pulled aside the curtain and watched him walk to his truck. She let out a shaky breath. She failed at keeping him away from her and Lucy today, she had let herself appear weak to him. It would never happen again, but how could she do that when this man gave her a million odd feelings.

Because he's a man and men are trouble and can never be serious. But Caleb was a good man to Candice and loved both

Lily and her. There just wasn't a good man for her and Lucy, it would be them against the world the rest of her life. Eli was just hanging around because she had custody of his niece. If he got Lily he'd have no reason to be around.

And she needed to remember that.

Chapter 7

Andie groaned when the four-a.m. alarm went off. She shut it off and slowly got up. She got into her typical bakery uniform, she headed over to the nursery where Lucy was just starting to stir.

She picked her up, changed her diaper, then did the same with Lily.

She took both girls out to the kitchen, she placed Lucy in her highchair since she was awake. Lily was still half asleep and snuggled into Andie's shoulder.

Andie got two bottles ready and went to get two jars of baby food, she managed to open the one jar still holding Lily. She set the jar on the other highchair and began to feed Lucy.

Lily slowly began to wake up more and Andie let out a small laugh. "Are you ready to eat, pretty girl?"

She let out a few babbles and rubbed her cheek against Andie's shoulder. She placed Lily in the other chair and got her to eat as well.

Soon she had them cleaned and ready to head over to the bakery. She began to walk over when a strange feeling washed over her. Her eyes darted around but she didn't see anything. She stood Lucy on the ground so she could unlock the door.

Andie propped the door open with her foot and scooped Lucy back up, locked the door, and headed to the playpen. She kissed each of their chunky cheeks and sat them down where they began to play.

She let out a sigh, grabbed the video monitor and began to bake her muffins, breads, scones, and other goodies.

After baking for a couple of hours she was ready to open. She flipped the sign to open, then began to load up the glass cases.

Ten minutes later everyone came rushing in to get their morning breakfast. She had debated on selling coffee or not when she first opened but when she tried to make some of the fancier coffee drinks it had been an epic fail.

So she stuck with what she knew. Candice and she had picked up baking when they were about ten. Rose had helped them at first, they would go to Candice's house every day after school to bake anything and everything. It was the only stable thing she had had in her life and now half of that stability was gone.

As she rushed around the shop to take care of her customers she got the same strange feeling she had when she and the girls headed over to the bakery that morning. A shiver ran down her spine as her eyes darted around. Nothing seemed unusual.

She pushed the feeling away and continued to serve her customers. As she was finishing up the last few customers the door opened again and Rose and Bruce enter the shop. She placed the fake smile on as they headed to Lucy and Lily.

The last customer finally left and Andie headed over to the Howells as they talked to Lily and Lucy. She smiled as she sat down beside them but kept quiet while they visited Lily.

Once she saw they were all okay she let out a sigh and began to clean up. This was her least favorite part of the day. But it needed to be done. She locked the door when it was becoming obvious a certain tall and very handsome cowboy wasn't coming by.

At the last wipe of her rag against the counter in the kitchen she heard a throat clear. She turned around and saw Bruce standing in the doorway. "Mr. Howell."

"Andie, we've known each other twenty years, when are you going to call us Bruce and Rose?" he sighed as he leaned against the frame.

"Sorry, sir, is everything okay with Lily and Lucy?" She felt her face heat up a smidge. She had never been allowed to call anyone by their first name unless they were closer to her age. She had never called an adult mom or dad, they were always, sir, ma'am, or Mr. and Mrs.

"Yeah, Rose and I want to talk to you before we head home today."

She threw the rag in the washer she had next to a dryer in the corner of the kitchen. "Sure, I just finished cleaning," she said and headed over to the metal swinging door, Bruce followed her.

They sat down on the empty pink cushioned chairs. "So, what's going on?" she asked as she looked at the older couple.

Bruce and Rose looked at each other then back to her. Rose reached out to grab her hand, and said, "Well, we and Maisy and Todd wanted to let you know we know why Candice and Caleb chose you and we agree. We're all too old to be running after a baby like Lily, she's always on the go now, we can just imagine how she'll be as a toddler and everything else, and we're proud of the way you stood your ground with Eli.

"We think once he realizes his dedication is to the ranch

and not to a baby he'll understand why Caleb and Candice chose you as well. He'll get over it, just keep standing your ground and don't let him scare you."

"He doesn't, he's got one hell of a temper but I'm not afraid of him," Andie said with determination. It was good to know Rose, Bruce, Maisy, and Todd supported the decision.

"Good, now the next part is we're thinking about trying to move closer, we have a lot to figure out but we want to be close to Lily, Lucy, and you so we can help you when you need it," Bruce said and reached out and squeezed her hand tightly. "And, if Eli Cameron gives you any trouble, you call me and I'll come set him straight."

Andie smiled a small smile. "Thank you."

"Are you sure there isn't anything else that you want?" Rose asked searching her eyes.

"Actually, there's an afghan Candice was making for Lily. I'd like to have it and if it's not finished, I'd like to finish it for her and give it to Lily when she's a little older."

"Was it pink?" Rose asked.

"Yes, and different greens, it was going to be camo."

"I know exactly where it is, come on, Bruce." Rose stood and picked up Lily who seemed okay with it.

Andie got Lucy and they left the bakery. They made their way to the U-Haul they had loaded up.

Rose directed Bruce to which box it was in and he managed to pull it out and then stepped out of the back of the U-Haul, closing the door.

He handed the afghan to Andie. "Thank you," she whispered as she took the somewhat dark pink blanket with the different shades of green in little circle clusters in diagonal lines. It looked finished.

Rose moved closer to her and hugged her tightly.

They headed back to her house.

Bruce and Rose kissed Lily and Lucy then hugged Andie. "If you need anything just call us," Rose whispered to her.

Andie nodded her head and watched as they headed out to the U-Haul and drove away.

Eli was out checking fences but his mind was on Andie and everything that was going on. He let out a heavy sigh. She'd let him hug her yesterday and touch her but that didn't mean he was in the clear from the way he had treated her the day they found out Caleb and Candice were gone and the day of the funeral at the house.

He ran a hand across his face and head, wiping the sweat from his brow. It was going to be a hot one today. He was debating on whether or not to go see them again today.

But he had an excuse, he had to deliver the pictures she wanted of her Lucy, Lily, and Candice. A smile touched his lips, yeah he wanted to see all three of them again.

He made his last round of the pastures and headed back to the barn. As he unsaddled his horse, Dale Hank came around the corner.

"Hey, boss, how are things?" he asked carefully.

Everyone knew how the littlest of things were setting him off. "Good, fences all look good, I've got to run a few things to Andie, so I'm going to head over there in a few."

"Okay, we'll handle everything here, give Lil a kiss for me," Dale called over his shoulder as he headed out of the barn running a hand over his short black hair.

Eli shook his head, it was crazy how close they had all gotten in the last year, the men were just as upset about Caleb and Candice.

They all wanted justice for the loving couple. He hated there was nothing he could do to get it.

Andie just finished feeding the girls, changing them, and laying them down for their naps. She changed into an old beat up pair of Sketchers, and had put on her dingy gray sweatpants, and a t-shirt that was just as old and ragged and had seen better days.

She headed out to the garage after grabbing the video monitor and checking on the girls one more time. She opened the door and got her red push mower out, checked the gas, then started it.

She began with the strip between her house and the bakery. She turned to make another swipe as the fresh-cut grass smell entered her nose. She jumped and let out a scream when she about hit Eli with the mower as he stood in her path.

He walked around the mower and made her shut it off. "What're you doing?"

"Mowing," she said and gestured, her voice had an *obviously* kind of tone.

"Well, I see that, where are the girls?"

"Inside, sleeping."

He raised a blond eyebrow.

She pulled the monitor off the side of her sweatpants, "See." She turned it toward him.

He looked over the monitor but he still had a scowl on his chiseled, unshaven face.

"What're you even doing here, Eli?" she demanded, pushing the excited feeling away that rushed over her trying to take away the disappointment she had felt when he hadn't shown up earlier.

He shrugged his shoulders a little. "I came to give you the pictures you wanted, then heard the mower, so I figured I would investigate." He walked closer to her and put one of his huge hands on the mower. "So, why don't you go inside and I'll finish this up?"

She rolled her eyes at him "Why don't you go inside and I'll finish it?"

"Because you put in a hard day at the bakery, and still have a full day with the girls. I'm free right now, so it makes perfect sense."

"I don't need help, Eli, I can do this. You've put in just as much work as me, if not more, I'm sure your jobs are not done there either." She went to take hold of the mower but he grabbed her hand gently.

Her eyes and head snapped up, why did he have to be so tall, and she so short? She barely came up to his chest and had to tilt her head pretty far back to look him in those yellowish, golden eyes of his.

He pulled her closer to him and laid his other hand against her back. "How about this is me making up for the two days I was an absolute dickhead to you?"

She narrowed her eyes at him. "Leaving me alone and not showing up to try to prove how irresponsible and unfit I am for Lily would be a perfect way to do that."

"Andie…"

"No, I'm not so stupid I don't know that's what you're trying to do here. I am not a bad mom to Lucy, so why would I be a bad mom to Lily? I know her pretty well. I can do this by myself, Eli," she explained.

"I know, but you don't have to."

"Why can't you accept that I want to?" she asked.

"Why can't you accept a nice gesture?"

"Men and nice gestures don't exist, it's all just a load of bull." She continued to glare up at him.

He pulled her even closer to him. She laid her hands against his hard chest, she about swooned but knew she couldn't.

"What about with Candice and Caleb? That kindness was real, he absolutely adored her and you know it," he challenged.

"Fine, kind gestures to *me* from men are a load of bull and nonexistent, and you do not adore me." She tried to push away from him again.

"That's because I was stupid and didn't take the opportunities that Caleb gave me. I'm not trying to prove you're bad for Lily, you love her. And, believe it or not, the opposite sex can be friends." He smiled still not letting go of her.

Her body began to react to his hard, toned one, a little over a year and half with no testosterone around could do that to a woman. Especially the kind this man put off. She could see it ooze from his powerful, resilient, muscles along his whole body. Like some Greek God. And that was just gathered from how he pressed her body up against his.

She took a deep breath. "But we're not friends, Eli. The day at the station was the first time we've talked since their wedding day and that wasn't a very long or intellectual conversation."

"Then, let's start over." It seemed more of a demand than a request. "By letting me mow both properties."

"Then will you go away?"

"Eh, guess you'll just have to find out, won't you?"

"Oh, you are so infuriating." She pushed from him and stormed back inside her house.

Eli chuckled as he watched the strong willed, spitfire storm away from him. He was sure she would have slammed the door if the girls hadn't been asleep.

Getting under her skin this way was a little fun. He had noticed the way her breath hitched when he got so close to her, the way her eyes had shone right before she shut her emotions off.

But no matter what it took or how much she would push him away he'd be there for her when she finally wanted and needed to break down.

Even a strong, determined, spitfire like herself would need to have the option. He turned to the mower and started it and took over from where she had stopped when he had scared her. Which he hadn't intended to do.

He got halfway done with the backyards and began to sweat. He unbuttoned his white, with light blue plaid lines, shirt after he turned the mower off and tossed it onto one of the plastic, white lawn chairs Andie had on the concrete patio and continued his work.

Andie checked on the girls then headed to the kitchen. Just because she was comfortable out in the heat didn't mean he was going to be.

She began to get out a pitcher from one of the oak cabinets. She filled it with cold water from her long, curved chrome faucet as she went to the pantry and pulled out the mix of pink lemonade.

It wouldn't be as good as fresh squeezed lemonade but it would have to do for today. She grabbed one of her plain drinking glasses from the cupboard, they were bigger than most glasses. She threw in some ice cubes then began to fill the glass with lemonade.

She made her way to the small sliding glass door that took her to the concrete patio off the back of her house. She stood there waiting for Eli to turn around to notice her. When he seemed to catch sight of her he changed direction and started mowing a strip that led him over to her.

Her eyes widened in shock as his tan skin glistened in the sun, his muscles rippled beneath his taut skin. She took a hard gulp at the sight of the muscles of his chest, the tightness of his abdomen that narrowed into lean hips and long, muscular thighs.

You could see everything ripple from his arms to his pectorals to those thighs of his, even though those were covered by jeans.

She felt her heart jump to her throat as he turned the mower and his rock-hard body came toward her. It took her a minute to find her voice as he tilted his brown Stetson up and hooked his thumbs into his front pockets. His light blue jeans hung on his hips a little and she couldn't help but follow the light blond hair that traveled from his navel and dipped into those jeans of his.

She licked her dry lips trying to moisten them. "I brought you some lemonade," she said, handing the glass to him. "There's more inside in the fridge if you want some more, you can help yourself," she whispered as he took the glass from her and she spun around quickly literally running back into the house.

She had never seen a man like him without a shirt on. Her face felt so hot as she pushed the door closed loudly. Her heart was beating a mile a minute.

She took off to her living room, he's just a man, an ass hat of a man, just don't get worked up over it, there is no way she would get sucked into his maleness, just because he had masculinity, unlike Daryl, did not mean she would fall into his arms harder than she had with him. She had learned her lesson and would never repeat her mistake.

She sat down on the couch and put the video monitor on the arm of the couch as she leaned against the comfy brown cushions. As she sat there her eyes began to get heavy and she slowly fell asleep, her head tilted back against the cushion behind her.

Eli finally had all of both yards done and he put the mower away in the garage and put the door down. He headed in from the garage house door and took the glass into the kitchen almost wanting to get another glass. He stopped when he heard the soft crying. He followed the sound to the living room.

When his sharp gaze landed on Andie, he rushed over to her and knelt in front of her. He shook her arm gently and said, "Andie, wake up."

Her eyes snapped open and she darted up from the couch, she tripped over her feet and landed into him knocking him down and landing on top of him. She pushed against him but he rolled her over and caught her hands in one fluid motion and pinned them against the floor.

"Let go of me," she demanded still struggling beneath his rock-hard body.

"Andie, just stop, it's okay, what happened?" he didn't move nor could either one of them break the eye contact.

"Just get off of me." She glared up at him those gray eyes changed in a flash like lightning to hard steel.

"Andie, it's okay, I'm not going to do anything. Was it a bad dream? What's wrong?"

"Nothing, Eli, leave me alone." She bucked her hips up beneath him and it sent his body a flame as her curves met his hard plains.

"Fine." He gave in and moved to his knees helping her up, he didn't need her feeling his instant desire for her.

"Are you done with the yard?" she demanded as she stood up and put a distance between them.

"Yes I am," he answered just as Lily began to cry.

She went to the nursery with him right behind her and Lucy began to wail a little.

He picked Lucy up and she got Lily. He followed her back out to the kitchen where she got two bottles ready for them. She handed one to Eli without even thinking and began to feed Lily.

Andie was so angry with herself. She had fallen asleep and was again plagued with the dreams. she couldn't get their bodies out of her mind no matter how hard she tried. It was becoming so normal to wake up after a few short hours of sleep in tears.

After the girls ate she turned to Eli. "Thanks, now you can go."

"Andie,"

"No, Eli, I don't want you here right now, I want to be left alone. Just let me call you later and stop coming by here unannounced, it's going to start a lot of drama and neither one of us need that right now, we can meet some where neutral and go from there for visits with Lily. Thanks for your help today but I really just need you to go."

His eyes hardened a little bit as he handed Lily over to her. "Fine." He headed out to the patio grabbed his shirt and left.

Andie put the girls down in the living room to play as Eli stormed from the house. Surprisingly, he didn't slam the door. She pulled the curtain back slowly and watched his muscles along his back work as he marched over to his truck. She didn't want an enemy in him, but she also couldn't keep letting him see her like this, it just wasn't going to be in her favor if he really tried to take Lily from her.

She needed to keep her distance from him there was no other way around this whole mess. It wasn't like she asked to be put in charge of Lily, she would do it to the best of her ability but she did not ask for it. And she didn't ask for him to come barging into her life either and the only reason he did was because she had his niece. Although he was very good with Lucy.

No, stop it, men are no good, and just because he's being sweet now does not mean a thing. Keep your distance from him. It's what needs done.

Chapter 8

A couple of days had gone by since Andie had seen Eli or heard from him. The days had gone pretty smoothly. She had gotten half of the order she had ordered a couple of days ago. Unfortunately, she was still waiting on the crib.

Before the girls had woken up from their daily nap she had parked her car a little more crooked in the driveway. Today she had to get the spark plugs and wires changed.

It was a beautiful day, not excruciatingly hot like the other day when she had wanted to mow and it wasn't chilly either. The girls were due to wake up soon. She began to get the baby food ready and the bottles, then she folded up the play and pack to put out under her huge maple tree, where the girls would be covered with the shade from the bunches of green leaves on the branches, while she worked on the car.

She headed back inside just as the girls began to wake up. She went to get them, changed their diapers, and headed out to the kitchen. She got them in their chairs and fed. She managed to get them out to the play and pack and settled. She found the wrench she'd need to loosen the spark plugs.

Something was churning in her gut, though, telling her to text Eli and ask if they could meet later. She needed to apologize for the other day but also wanted to get him to understand why she didn't want him hanging around so much.

If she, by some miracle, let him in, would he break her heart? Because who wanted to be with someone who still wasn't supposed to be able to have kids? Lucy had been a blessing and a miracle.

After her check-up, the doctors were so surprised and amazed she had carried Lucy to full term and that she was still so healthy.

She took a deep breath as she grabbed her phone off the hood of the car and typed the text. *If you want to come see Lily today, that'd be fine, just let me know where you'd want to meet and I'll be there.* She went to the driver's side and popped the hood and laid her phone on the front seat since the outfit she was wearing didn't have anywhere she could hold her phone. She had opted for a skinny strapped black tank top and shorts that didn't have any pockets but they were both so beat up it didn't matter if she ruined them while working on the car.

She smiled as she watched the girls play as she lifted the hood. She began to dive into the work that needed to be done to her car, hoping Eli would text her back by the time she was finished. She didn't expect her task to take too long.

Eli felt his pocket vibrate, he slowly pulled it out of his pocket as he threw the last scoop of dirty manure into the wheelbarrow.

He unlocked his phone and went to his messages. Andie was the one he had a new message from. And for some stupid reason he could do nothing but smile and it got even bigger as he read the text.

He hurriedly replied, *We don't have to go anywhere, I don't care what the idiots in this town want to say, you're taking care of my niece, that's the only excuse they need to know why I am at your house so much, I'll be there in ten.*

He grabbed the wheelbarrow, dumped it, and headed inside to get cleaned up. He shot a text to Dale to let him know where he was going and got an, *Okay, boss,* as the reply.

He headed to his truck and made his way into town. He couldn't wait to see Lily, Lucy, and Andie. It had almost killed him to stay away the last couple of days but he knew he had to give her space at the same time.

He just hoped this move proved he didn't care what anyone else would say about him and her being around each other.

He was getting a little nervous. He finally pulled up outside of Andie's house, he was a little confused when he saw her car was parked a little crooked in her driveway.

He got out of the truck quickly and rushed over to the car when he heard her yelling.

"You stupid, stubborn, piece of junk, come on!"

He walked closer and saw the hood was up and Andie was kneeling on top of the edge of the frame, leaning over the back of the engine a little.

"Oh you dumb thing, you're the last one I have to get off!" she yanked harder and he heard the pop as he moved closer behind her and she went sprawling backwards off the car.

Before she fell he managed to grab a hold of her hips, steadying her on the frame.

She let out a scream and turned her head back toward him.

"What're you doing?" he asked and raised an eyebrow at her. Her eyes seemed to sparkle a little at the sight of him.

"Fighting with spark plug wires," she mumbled.

He raised his eyebrow even further, "Would you like some help?"

She sighed as he picked her up from the hood and set her

feet on the ground., "Sure, why not? I'm not in the mood to argue right now." She moved out of his way and leaned against the car facing the play and pack as the girls babbled to each other.

Eli hadn't expected her to admit to not being in any kind of mood. He yanked off his hat and pulled his white t-shirt off leaving himself in only a gray tank top and his darker jeans. He placed his hat on top of her head pushing it down over her eyes a little.

She looked back to him and tilted it up a little.

He took in a sharp breath, man, that had probably been a bad idea, she looked so sexy in his hat. He swallowed hard and turned to the hood of the car and began to take out the spark plugs. "Is it safe to assume you need the oil changed as well?"

"Yeah, but I'm doing that tomorrow. Who knows how long the girls will be okay being confined to the play and pack?"

He glanced over to where she was looking. He smiled at the sight. Those two got along so well. At least now they would have each other. He turned back to work under the hood. "I could change it while I'm here, then if they get restless you could take them inside," he suggested.

He glanced at Andie as she shrugged her shoulders. "Whatever, what happened to meeting somewhere so you could see Lily?"

"Makes more sense for me to come here, then you dragging two babies around the whole county just for me to spend a little time with her, didn't you get my text?"

"Um, no, my phone is in the car, I don't have any pockets and didn't expect a text back before I was done." She glanced at him then went around to the driver's side of the car. He could barely take his eyes off of her in that skimpy tank top and tight shorts. She knew how to get his blood boiling without even trying.

He tore his gaze from her and began to switch out the spark plugs.

———

Andie felt the butterflies in her stomach. All because of Elijah Cameron. She'd never felt this before because of a man but why'd it have to be that man? The minute he sensed trouble he would take Lily before she had time to blink.

She opened the door and grabbed her phone as she sunk into the gray cushioned seat. She glanced over to check the girls again and they were still okay.

She looked back to her phone and opened the message from Eli. She began to read it as she tilted his hat up on her head a little.

She locked her phone and got out of the car when the chill ran up her spine again. She turned around quickly as the hair along her arms stood on end.

Her eyes flicked around quickly, nothing was there. Nothing was different. She looked over to Lily and Lucy and they seemed fine. She rushed around the back of the car as her eyes moved fast, looking around. All of a sudden she didn't feel comfortable being outside at all.

Lucy pulled herself up as Andie got closer to them. Lily did, too. She picked them up quickly and headed toward the house.

"Andie?" Eli called out to her.

She turned toward him but didn't say anything. Her eyes were glued to him as he walked up to her. She almost whimpered when he laid his hand against her arm.

"Hey, what's wrong?" he asked, concern written on his handsome face.

"I-I don't know, I just feel better having the girls inside."

He reached out to help her and Lucy went into his arms.

"Okay, c'mon let's get you guys inside." He held Lucy in one arm and moved her toward the door.

She moved closer to him, feeling safe from the unknown threat she was feeling. He wrapped his arm around her tightly. She looked at him from under her eyelashes. This was going to be a conversation between them, she could already feel it coming.

She reached for the knob and turned it, he let her go in first. This was just going to give him more cause to take Lily. Maybe he'd let it go?

As soon as he shut the door his arm wrapped around her again taking her into the living room. He placed Lucy on the floor and Lily, then moved her to the couch and knelt in front of her. He tilted the hat up, so it wasn't hiding her eyes.

As he moved it, her eyes locked with his golden ones. "What happened out there, Andie?"

She was so afraid to tell him but knew he had a right to know. "Do you ever get the feeling you're being watched?" she whispered as she looked at Lucy and Lily as they crawled to their toys.

"Not particularly, is that what you felt?" he laid a hand on her bare knee which made her look at him.

She nodded her head a little. "It's the third time it's happened this week, the first time happened twice the day Rose and Bruce left and just now."

He moved to sit on the couch and made her turn her body toward him a little as he glanced out the huge bay window behind the couch., "Who do you think would be watching you?"

Their eyes locked together. The only person she could think of was Daryl but that would make no sense. No one knew where she went when she left North Dakota because there was no one to tell. "I honestly don't know, Eli, no one knows where I am because I had no one to tell, except Rose and Bruce but there's not really anyone who would try to find me."

Eli looked at Lucy for a minute as she squealed and began to chew on her ring of keys. "What about Lucy's dad?"

Andie shivered at the thought and actually moved closer to Eli. "God, I hope not, last I knew he was with someone else," she whispered.

He put an arm around her. "Okay, look I'm sure we'll figure it out, for now why don't you stay in here with the girls? I'll finish the car, change the oil, then we can get some food. I don't want to leave you alone right now, so I'll stay until you feel comfortable."

All she did was nod her head, but the sad part was she didn't know if she'd feel comfortable later. She took a deep breath when he stood up from the couch. She watched him leave out the door but she already wanted him near her again. She sighed and bit her lip as she closed her eyes tightly. *Don't be such a silly woman, you'll be fine, you're stronger than this, don't let the lack of sleep and stress get to you.*

She got down on the floor and played with Lucy and Lily. She tried to push the uneasy feeling away. She felt a little better that Eli was there but what would happen when he went home?

Whatever it would be, she would face it head-on, she would not show more weakness than she already had.

Eli's eyes darted around as he walked out of the house. He didn't see anything, but he wasn't going to doubt Andie, something had definitely spooked her.

He headed to the car and quickly finished the plugs and wires. Did he dare to do the oil? He didn't want to be away from Andie and the babies much longer but it needed taken care of. He was sure he could do it quickly.

He looked in the garage and found the oil pan and headed back to the car. He found the oil she had bought and the filter. He couldn't lie, her knowing how to do these things for her car was an even bigger turn on.

He let a smile touch his lips as he grabbed the filter and oil then went under the car. There was just enough room for him to squeeze underneath. He pulled out the plug and unscrewed the filter. He kept his ears alert while he let the oil drain.

His mind began to wander, what if Andie's ex was here? What if he suddenly wanted something to do with Lucy? That made his blood hot, over his dead body. He didn't know a whole lot about her ex but any man who would abandon her and his daughter was a worthless pig and Lucy and Andie both deserved better. Hell they deserved better than his hot-headed ass. Not that it had even been discussed and he didn't even know what he was really feeling toward her.

The oil finally stopped draining and he replaced the plug then the filter. He got out from under the car and his eyes darted around again. Still no one stood out to him.

He filled the car up with the new oil and dropped the hood. He pulled the oil pan from under the car and began to put it in the empty jug. He found a marker in the garage and wrote used on it then set it on the floor. He'd get rid of it later.

He shut the garage door as a UPS truck pulled up in front of his. The man began to get out and went to the back and pulled out a semi-thick, long, and wide box.

Eli went out to him. "Need some help with that?"

"Sure, thanks."

Eli grabbed the other side and they began to walk up to the door. "Thanks, I think I can get it inside."

The UPS man nodded his head and left to go back to his

truck. Eli waited for him to start driving away before he opened the door.

He pulled the box inside the house. "Special delivery!" he called out as he shut the door.

Andie poked her head out from the living room. "Oh, the crib," she said excitedly, she headed back to get the girls and came back out one on each hip. "Do you need help getting it to the bedroom?" she asked her gray eyes meeting his.

"Nope, I got it." He began to push the box down the hallway and into the nursery. He was already opening it by the time Andie came into the room and put the girls in the white crib that was already in there.

"I'll be right back, I have to get the play and pack." She began to leave the bedroom but he caught her hand turning her back to him.

"Why don't you stay in here, I'll get it." He tilted his hat up, that she was still wearing, so he could see her face better without the shadow.

"Are you sure?"

He tilted his hat up a little more. "Yeah I'm sure, I'll be right back." He brushed her jaw with his forefinger gently then headed out to get the play and pack.

He got it quickly and put it back in the living room and headed back to the nursery. He let out a chuckle when he found Andie amongst the parts of the new crib, sitting Indian style, still wearing his hat, and reading the instructions to the crib.

He went over to sit beside her amongst the parts and glanced at the instruction pictures. "I still say you should have taken the one from the house, it would have been a lot easier."

She shot a look at him, her eyebrows raised so far they went beneath his hat. "I would have had to hook it up to my car and drag it here, it would have been ruined."

He nudged her shoulder with his. "Yeah, because you don't

know a cowboy with a long bed truck who could have gotten it here and has the man power to get it inside this tiny house."

She pursed her lips for a minute. "Well, that cowboy with that long bed is trying to take Lily back, so my trust for him is limited," she tossed out at him as she looked back to the instructions.

He snatched the paper out of her hands and with a finger on her chin gently turned her head to look at him. "I want you to listen to me, and listen good. I'm not taking Lily away. I was pissed off at first between the lack of sleep I had gotten, and the grief we've both been enduring. I couldn't understand why they chose you, one day I will understand better because you'll tell me why, because I think deep down you know why they chose you."

She looked away quickly as she tried to hide the tears that clearly formed in her eyes. She moved to start putting pieces together.

He began to help her.

An hour later, and a few snappy comments between them, they finally got the crib together. They moved it on to the wall across from Lucy's crib, put the new mattress in it, and Andie got some sheets for it.

She was too short to slip the sheet on, so Eli did it with ease.

Lily let out a squeal making Andie and Eli turn to her and she held out her hands to them. Andie stood back and let Eli get her.

She smiled as Lily snuggled her head against his shoulder. He kissed her cheek as Lucy stood and bounced in the crib a little then held her hands up to Eli.

He didn't hesitate and picked her up and she snuggled against his other shoulder and he kissed her cheek as well.

Andie bit back a sigh and started to clean up the mess she and Eli had made.

He had really set her mind to working on why Candice and Caleb had chosen her. There could have been so many reasons or none whatsoever. Maybe because she knew what it was like never knowing her parents? Never knowing what being loved felt like?

All she knew was hate and disgust from people, so no, she didn't know what a parent's love felt like. She saw Rose and Bruce with Candice, so she saw their love. And she just knew to do what they would have done or just the complete opposite of what had been done to her.

She managed the clean-up and got the box out to the garage. She pulled Eli's hat off of her head as she walked back into the house.

There was so much Eli probably deserved to know but she wasn't ready to tell him. She honestly didn't know if she would ever be ready to tell him everything about her life.

"Hey, why'd you take the hat off?" his voice broke her train of thought.

She looked up seeing him with both girls, she walked forward to take Lucy and placed his hat on his head, even though she loved seeing him without it and she could feast her eyes on his multi-shade of blond hair. It was light but had darker, and natural highlights through it. She wondered what it would be like to tangle her fingers through it, and how soft it actually was.

Andie cleared her throat a little. "I just figured you'd want it back before you left," she murmured as she settled Lucy in her arms.

He slid his now free arm around her shoulders. "Yeah, I

guess, but we're still having supper, would pizza pique your interest?"

"Sure." She kept her answer short and sweet, even though there were quite a few other things that were piquing her interest at the moment.

They took the girls to their highchairs and sat them in it, Andie went to the pantry to get their finger snacks when Eli snapped his fingers.

He pulled his hat off and placed it back on her head. "I'll be right back, I need to get you those pictures you wanted out of my truck and I have something else you might want. Keep that, I like how it looks on you, what do you want on your pizza?"

"Anything but anchovies, mushrooms, and pepperoni."

"Okay."

All she could do was watch him leave like a streak of lightning.

She shook her head and gave the girls their snacks and went to get the baby food. She'd make them bottles after they ate.

Chapter 9

li darted outside, grabbed his shirt off the mirror of Andie's car then headed to his truck. He called the pizza parlor and ordered their pizza for delivery and paid, including a tip, with his card.

He grabbed the photo and the other item he had picked to give to Andie. He shut the door and darted his eyes around again, but he still didn't see anything that would set Andie off.

He headed inside the house and made his way back to the kitchen. He set the items he brought in and his shirt on the table as he took a seat in a chair and dove in to helping Andie feed the girls.

They finished eating then he and Andie cleaned them up. Eli took Lily and she took the bottle.

Andie took Lucy and they headed to the living room, they sat beside each other on the leather brown couch as the girls finished their bottles.

"So, how is Lily doing?" Eli asked as he gazed into her little golden eyes.

"She has her moments. I know she misses them, but she

doesn't understand, when she's older I'll try my best to explain to her what happened. She'll need you to tell her about Caleb and she'll need me to tell her about Candice." They looked at each other at the same time.

"We'll make it work." He smiled at her then there was a knock on the door.

He handed Lily to Andie and headed to the door, he grabbed the pizza and went back to Andie. "Where do you want to eat?"

"In here is fine." she adjusted both girls who were done with their bottles. "They can play while we eat, then it'll be bath time."

He wanted to jump to help but he didn't want to overdo it either. He set the box down on the cushion. "Do you have paper plates?"

"I think so, check the cabinet above the microwave."

He headed into the kitchen, grabbed the paper plates and two cokes, along with the stuff he had brought in a little bit ago.

He made his way back to Andie and the girls. He smiled when he saw Lily and Lucy on the floor playing. He handed a plate to Andie and they each took some pizza. He noticed she only took a couple of slices, so he took a couple more and put them on her plate.

She didn't say anything, surprisingly, she ate slowly. But she managed to eat it all.

They leaned back against the couch letting their food settle. He picked up the items he'd wanted to give her. He handed the two things to her. "I know you wanted this, but I also found this and I figured you'd want that too."

She took the picture frame and Lily's baby book. "Oh, Eli, thank you." Her fingers ran across the pink, sparkly book with butterflies.

She put the book in her lap and wrapped her arms around his neck and hugged him tightly.

He hugged her back, one hand pressed against her back, the other cupped the back of her head.

She slowly pulled back from him and their eyes locked, her eyes seemed to look deeply into him. "I better give the babies their baths and get them ready for bed."

His hands slid from her body slowly. "I could help," he whispered.

"Okay." She gave in to him with ease. She picked up the book and frame and Lily while he took the pizza and put it in the fridge. He came back and picked up Lucy and followed Andie.

She went to the nursery first, got jammies, and diapers for them. Then he followed her to her bedroom.

He glanced around, the room was an off white, just a plain dresser, small bed that wasn't on any special kind of frame. Everything looked so plain, as if she didn't want something to show her personality or didn't want to get attached to any possessions.

But Lucy and Lily's room was a gorgeous lavender purple, all white furniture, and stuffed animals galore. He didn't understand it.

He let out a sigh and followed her into the just as plain bathroom. He watched her bend over a little and turn on the tub.

She let the water run for a minute then put the stopper in the drain. She let the tub fill up a little. "Have you ever given Lil a bath before?"

"Twice," he answered snapping his eyes away from her ass, looking up and letting out a sigh of relief when he saw she hadn't turned her head to look at him.

But then she turned and grabbed two fluffy blue towels.

She shut the water off and knelt on the black and white tiled floor. She switched him Lily for Lucy and began to strip her after she laid her down on the towel. She picked Lucy up and sat her toward the back of tub.

Eli wasn't sure how this was going to work at first. She glanced back at him for a second as Lucy began to splash.

"Are you going to get Lily ready or do you want me to?"

"I've got it," he answered and laid Lily down on the towel. He got her undressed and moved beside Andie. His nose was filled with that rose, vanilla, and sugar scent again.

It caused an ache deep inside him. Maybe all of this was a bad idea. How could he be feeling this rush of desire when he had just lost his brother not even a week ago. And she sure as hell couldn't be feeling anything because that was just Andie. She shut all her emotions and feelings off.

He had been with a few women before but none of them had affected him like this.

He swallowed hard and placed Lily in the tub. It didn't take them very long to bathe the girls. Andie pulled the towels toward them with her foot. She held Lucy with one hand while she handed him a towel then grabbed the other one.

She wrapped Lucy and he got Lily, they headed to the bedroom after she pulled the plug in the tub and grabbed the baby lotion, which was on the vanity top in the bathroom, along with the clothes and diapers.

His gaze hardly left Andie for a minute as they laid the girls down on the bed but then he needed to get Lily dried.

His shook his head, why was she suddenly affecting him so damn bad?

She finished with the lotion then handed it to him. Their fingers brushed as he took it from her. She still felt a little cold. He wanted to ask her about it but doubted he'd get an answer.

They finished with the girls and headed back to the nursery. Andie kissed Lucy on the cheek. "I love you, sweetie." She laid her down gently and covered her with her favorite blanket.

He watched her walk over to him and Lily, she kissed Lily on the cheek also. "And I love you, cutie."

Eli kissed Lily and laid her down in the crib and covered her as well.

Andie flipped on their nightlight and headed toward the door. As soon as he was out behind her she pulled the door shut a little.

They headed to the front door. As she stopped off to the side of the door he stepped closer to her.

"Do you feel okay to stay here by yourself?" he asked quietly.

Andie's gaze locked with his, her heart about melted at the question. But she froze it back up. He'd been decent to her today, so what? It was only because they were trying to make things work for Lily's sake.

And Lily would be the only reason for their contact.

She took a deep, shaky breath. "I'll be fine, so will the girls, I'll make sure of it."

He seemed to study her closely but he nodded his head, he ran the back of his fingers against her cheek gently. "If you get worried at all I can be here in ten minutes, five if I rush."

She nodded her head as his thumb brushed her cheek bone. For a fleeting moment she thought he was going to kiss her. She saw his beautiful golden eyes darken a little and flick from her eyes to her lips then back to her eyes.

And for that short moment she wanted him to, but instead he backed away placing his hand on the knob. She turned to the door and locked the deadbolt and the knob lock. She let out a hard, shaky breath as she laid her forehead against the white painted door. She closed her eyes tightly.

She hated herself, she couldn't let him in, he would want a family, one he could start, not an already made family. Or maybe he didn't want one at all, he had been so dedicated to starting up his ranch and it was still a big part of him. It was still coming up off the ground a little.

She hated to admit she had felt alive with him so close to her today. She had felt the same way at the wedding and it couldn't happen.

If she let her guard down with him, he was sure to break her all over again. It had already stung when he hadn't given her the time of day when Candice and Caleb had gotten married.

Then again, he had probably known she was pregnant then and the only reason he was giving in now was because she had Lily. Why couldn't she remember that? She had to start. And now.

She finally managed to pull herself away from the door turning the lights out as she headed to go take her shower and then be off to bed

Being alone was what worked for her and she had to keep it that way. She didn't want broken. Again.

Eli pulled his hat low over his eyes as they darted around one last time. Nothing. Damn. Was everything getting to Andie? No, there was no way.

She held herself together for the girls. He'd never forget the way she had shivered when he had mentioned Lucy's dad.

There was something there, he just knew it. Just being left wouldn't cause her to tremble like that. He got up into his truck and sat there as he watched the lights shut off inside the little gray house in every room except her bedroom. He sighed as he began to wonder what all she had hidden about her ex.

He started the truck and began to head home. Now he knew he'd be back tomorrow just to check on them.

Something was starting to eat at his stomach and it wasn't good.

Chapter 10

E li was checking the fences. Again. You never could do enough fence checking on a ranch. He had woken up this morning with the same gut churning feeling that had plagued him last night, up until he fell asleep at the miserable midnight hour.

Between the gut churning feeling and the guilt that was settling deep inside him. He should still be mourning his brother and sister-in-law. He shouldn't have felt the happiness he had felt last night, but Andie seemed to pull it out of him without even trying.

His parents were still so upset about Caleb and he didn't blame them. He was upset too, but one woman and two little girls made it disappear a little.

He'd just been there last night and he wanted to be with all three of them already. Part of him had been glad Andie hadn't called him last night but the other part was a little hurt and upset. He knew she couldn't feel that at ease all of a sudden. She was burying it again. Just like she always did.

Ugh. What was he thinking? He was never going to talk to his brother ever again and it hurt, but there was nothing he could do about it. But he could keep himself from becoming a mechanical robot like everyone else had done around him. Everyone but Andie.

She could have become robotic but she didn't for the girls, and he was admiring it about her instead of being upset like he had been the day they had found out about his family.

He needed that un-robotic interaction. Someone who wasn't going to tiptoe around him.

He made another round of the fences then headed back to the barn where he took care of his horse and sent him out to the pasture. He headed inside to get freshened up.

Sure his clothes had the permanent smell of hay, horses, and leather soap, but that didn't mean he couldn't try to smell clean.

He finished, went out to his truck and headed to Andie's. Something twisted in his gut and he didn't know why.

He pulled up into her driveway beside her car and anger seeped through him when his eyes landed on Andie.

"Andie, what are you doing?" he demanded seeing her fidget on the ladder as he came up to the side of it.

Andie put the girls down for their naps after she fed them. She'd changed into a pair of black shorts and a purple tank top and headed out to the garage to get her ladder, she leaned it against the gutter of the house in the front. She would slowly make her way around the house.

She hadn't felt the hair standing feeling all day so she figured she'd be okay to get her gutters cleaned out. She'd grabbed her garden hose, hooked it up, and began to climb up the ladder.

She'd gotten up on the eighth rung when her foot got

tangled in the hose. She let out an aggravated sigh and began to try to get her foot out of the hose.

She was holding onto the ladder by one hand and had her untangled foot on the rung while trying to yank off the hose.

She didn't notice the ladder sliding against the gutter a little.

The deep voice below her scolded her, making her jump and the ladder began to slide off the gutter sideways.

She screamed as she fell into a hard body and wrapped her arms around their neck tightly. They both tumbled to the ground and the ladder crashed beside them.

She pushed back when she heard the loud oof from below her.

Gray met amber, even though her face was somewhat covered with her hair. She felt a hand run up her side and to her hair, brushing it back behind her ear.

"Andie, what were you trying to do?" the unmistakable voice asked as they stared at each other.

"My gutters need cleaned out and I got wrapped up in the stupid hose."

Eli slowly rolled so she was on her back. "And was that such a good idea?" he asked as he searched her eyes. Then those eyes moved to her lips.

"It was a good idea, actually, until I got my foot stuck and you scared me." Her eyes involuntarily looked to his lips. Both of their breaths seemed to hitch a little bit as their eyes collided together again.

She licked her dry lips and tried to swallow. Her breath became faster and shallower as his thumb brushed against her cheekbone like the night before.

"Are you at least okay?"

She was only able to nod her head as she was captured by those rare eyes of his.

as he had thought she would. Like pure sugar, as if she had been made for him.

Then right before he sent her inside he'd kissed her again and it felt, well, right. Maybe if he had taken the time to get to know her, like Caleb had wanted, they might be together now. Maybe nothing would have happened to his brother and sister-in-law.

Maybe they all would have been a happy family? He let out a groan as he came up between the last two houses. Nothing. He made his way back to Andie and the girls.

He rushed into the house and began to panic a little when he couldn't find Andie. He rushed to the nursery and let out a sigh of relief when he found all three of his girls safe.

His girls? Two kisses and he already thought of them as his? With Lily it made sense. With Andie and Lucy not so much. He checked on the girls then knelt in front of Andie.

She looked so lost sitting there with her head in her hands, he slowly pulled her hands away and lifted her up into his arms. He took her to her bedroom then the bathroom. He turned the water on and began to fill it up.

"Andie, why don't you take a bath? I'll keep an eye out and keep an ear open for the girls, I'll do the gutters later." He touched her shoulder gently as she just watched the tub fill with water.

She looked at him slowly, her bottom lip began to tremble a little. "Okay," she whispered.

He squeezed her shoulder. Which wasn't enough. He pulled her into his arms and held her tight for a few moments. He wanted to kiss her again but fought the urge. He let her go and turned to go to the living room.

He sat on the couch sideways, his back pressed against the arm of the couch and stared out the huge bay window. Begging for something to catch his eye. Still nothing.

He let out a groan, scrubbed his face with his rough hands, and threw his Stetson to the other side of the couch.

He didn't care how much Andie protested, he would be staying the night. Maybe if whoever this person was, who gave her the creeps, would see his truck in the driveway overnight and back off.

He stretched his one leg on the couch and placed his other foot on the floor. This couch wasn't going to be comfy but he'd make do. He was not leaving them alone tonight.

Andie let out a sigh as she sank a little further in the water. She'd be lying to herself if she said she wasn't scared.

Why was she feeling so many things all at once? Fear, loneliness, sadness, and a dug up want for the uncle of the little girl she had been given guardianship over.

She heard a little grunt on the monitor and she knew the girls were waking up. She pulled the plug on the tub.

She had been so good at hiding every emotion she'd ever felt because that was what had been beaten into her. Seen, not heard. And every time she made herself be heard once too many times she'd be shipped somewhere else.

No one ever thought she was worth anything, except Candice. And she was gone. She got out of the tub, wrapped herself in a towel, and rushed to the nursery and scooped Lily up and went to get Lucy as Eli walked in.

He froze for a minute as his gaze raked over her. He began to walk closer to her and the girls. "I'll get them, Andie. I told you I would."

"It's okay, really, I shouldn't have even tried to indulge in the bath."

"Yes, you should have, it's not going to be the end of the

world if you let me step in for a little bit and help out." He took Lucy and Lily out of her arms.

She let him take them and part of her hoped he'd lean down and kiss her in the process but he didn't. She couldn't keep thinking like this. She couldn't let him keep trying to become part of her life. She was a loner and the creepy feeling she kept having didn't mean he had a right to pull her out of the loner path she had created for herself.

"Go, Andie, it's okay." He moved aside to let her walk out of the nursery and she did because she couldn't keep standing in front of him stupidly in only a towel.

She rushed to her room and finished drying off then got dressed in a pair of gray sweatpants and a blue tank top and black bra and panties. She went to the nursery where she saw Eli just finishing up with getting Lucy redressed. "Is Lily done?" she asked quietly.

"Yes, she is," he replied. He stood up and took both girls with him as he went to the kitchen to get them their snacks. She followed him and watched as he placed first Lily in her chair then Lucy and then fastened them both in.

She bit her bottom lip hard, he would have been just as capable of taking care of Lily. Why had Candice and Caleb done this to him? He loved Lily and would have put her first every single day. She let out a sigh as she headed over to help him.

Eli heard the sigh and he turned towards her. "What's wrong?" he asked gently as he placed the girls' snacks on their tables.

"I'm sorry, Eli."

He frowned at her and pulled her down into his lap as he sat down in one of the wooden kitchen chairs. "For what?"

"You had more of a right to get Lily, I know you would

have taken care of her, you're great with her, I don't know why Candice and Caleb chose me and I'm sorry." She turned away from him so he couldn't see her eyes, but it was too late he had already seen them filling up with tears.

He gently tilted her head to his and his eyes searched hers. "It's okay, they knew I was so dedicated to the ranch, they didn't think I was ready to take care of a baby, she's safe with you and you love her as much as I do." He rubbed her cheek gently with his thumb. "Please don't cry, we're figuring this out and so far it's okay. Except for you falling off the ladder," his voice became serious and stern, "no more doing that stuff. You have two little girls to think about, what if something had happened and I hadn't been there to catch you?" he asked. "I'm serious, Andie, I better not catch you doing something like that again because there will be consequences. Do you understand?"

She swallowed hard. "I'm not sure what you mean exactly." Which wasn't entirely the truth, she was pretty sure he was talking about spanking her. Who knew Eli was like the heroes in the books she loved to read?

"You put yourself in danger and you won't be sitting comfortably for quite a while. Do you understand now?" he asked, while watching her intently.

"Yes, sir," she squeaked. Sir? Where did that come from?

"Have we settled things now?" he enquired.

She shrugged her shoulders. "Yes, but what if this stupid feeling doesn't go away, what if they are in danger?" She looked to the girls.

He pulled her into him closer and wrapped his arms around her as she laid her head against his shoulder. "We'll do everything we can to protect them, Andie, nothing is going to happen. I'm staying here with you guys tonight, hopefully if they see my truck in the driveway all night, they'll realize you have someone else on your side and will just disappear."

She let out a shaky breath. "You don't have to stay, Eli, really."

"That's not up for discussion, I am staying no matter how much you fight me. I am making sure my ladies stay safe tonight."

"And where will you sleep?"

"The couch. I've already made up my mind about this, we'll let the girls finish their snacks, and let them have some play time. Then we'll fix supper, get them ready for bed, just like last night, the only difference is I'm not leaving."

She searched his eyes for a minute and seemed to give in. That was proof enough to him that she was actually scared and this was the closest he was going to get to her admitting it.

They did exactly as Eli had said they were going to do. They managed to scrape together a nice warm chili soup and some corn bread. After they fed the girls and fed themselves they got the girls settled down for the night and they headed back out to the living room for a little bit.

The tension that hung between them was almost stifling. Andie wanted to ask Eli about those two kisses so bad but she was so scared to ask at the same time. She was caught off guard when he sat on the couch sideways and pulled her down between his muscular thighs. He wrapped his arms around her shoulders and pulled her back against his chest.

She felt her body began to warm as his warmth soaked into her. She laid her head back against his shoulder a little, "Eli, I didn't think I was ever in trouble, I've never felt this until that day Rose and Bruce left."

"I believe you, it's going to be okay, Andie, I'm here to help. I guess I'm making up for being such an ass hat, I know it's not near enough but I'll slowly make up for it."

She turned a little and laid her head against his chest, "I wish Candice was here, she'd know what to do, and I could leave Lucy with her while I try to figure this out."

He rubbed her back gently and kissed the top of her head. "I could see if my parents will watch them for a little bit?" he suggested.

"Maisy and Todd would watch Lily with no problem, Lucy would be another story, she's not their granddaughter. I would never ask them to watch her since she's nothing to them."

He sighed but continued to hold her and rub her back, her eyes slowly began to close as she snuggled against his chest more and held onto his shirt.

Eli felt her body relax in his arms, he looked down and saw she was asleep. He kissed her forehead gently. He let out a sigh as Andie snuggled closer. He turned to look out the window behind the couch. Something out there was scaring Andie and he didn't know what to do. The cops would want proof before they did anything. They wouldn't just go off of gut instinct or a feeling.

He managed to get a better hold of Andie in his arms and carried her to her bedroom. He laid her down on her bed and slowly covered her up. He switched the alarm on and put her phone on the charger. He kissed her forehead gently and brushed her cheek with his knuckles letting out another soft sigh.

He went back to the living room, kicked his boots off, and lay down on the couch. This was going to be a very long night he decided as he tried to get comfortable. His legs were scrunched up and he was almost falling off the edge. But it would be worth it to keep his girls safe.

Chapter 11

Eli jerked awake when he heard the scream and stumbled from the couch quickly. He rushed back to the bedrooms. He checked the girls first and they were sleeping peacefully.

He went to Andie's room and spotted her right away, standing in front of the small window. He walked up to her slowly. "Andie?"

She spun around quickly.

With the soft glow from the bedside lamp he could see how pale she was, her eyes wide with fear, and she was shaking.

He walked up to her as he glanced at the digital alarm clock. Two forty-five. He reached her and she moved into him wrapping her arms around him and laid her head just below his chest, "What's wrong?" he asked as he rubbed her back and cradled her head.

"Must have just been a bad dream," she mumbled into his shirt.

"Do you want to talk about it?"

She began to tremble a little more. "It's the same dream I've been having since the night at the station, only it shifted to something different, someone was standing outside my window and looking... Oh, no, the girls!" She pulled away but he pulled her back to him.

"Easy, Andie, they're okay. I checked on them before I came in here, I wanted to make sure you weren't in there." He rubbed her shoulders a little. "Why don't you try to get a little more sleep?"

Her eyes darted to the clock and let out a loud, heavy sigh. "There's no point, it's already three. I have to be up in half an hour to get a shower and get the girls ready so I can start baking."

"I could stay and watch them today if you'd like me to," he offered pulling her back against him.

"It's okay, Eli, you have the ranch to worry about, I can handle the girls." She pulled away but not before he saw the tears brimming her soft gray eyes. She grabbed some clothes and rushed into the bathroom.

"Andie," he called but she just shut the door. He took a deep breath. He didn't know what to do, part of him wanted to go after her, part of him knew she wanted space.

He opted for giving her space. So much had happened in the last week. But he wasn't leaving until he helped her get Lily and Lucy to the bakery.

He headed to the kitchen to start a pot of coffee.

Andie took a fast shower, got herself ready for work then headed to get the girls. The scent of fresh coffee swirled around her. It smelled so delicious but she didn't think she'd give in to the temptation.

Her on coffee, with the little sleep she had been getting was a disastrous idea. She went to get the girls up and ready then headed to the kitchen.

She stopped dead when she saw Eli standing in her little kitchen. Would she ever get used to how much room he took up?

He turned around as if he felt her presence and set the black coffee mug on the counter. He walked to her, took Lucy and placed her in the highchair while Andie put Lily in the other. Lily was slowly getting used to the schedule of waking up so early in the morning.

Andie hated doing it to her but didn't have a choice. She had placed an ad for a babysitter for Lucy with no luck a while ago. Who would take care of two girls?

She went to get the jars of baby food while Eli adjusted the chairs in front of the girls, like he'd been doing it forever. She took in a deep breath and headed back to them.

She and Eli began to feed them. Soon they were drinking their bottles and Eli helped her clean up. He then helped her get Lily and Lucy over to the bakery.

He kissed the girls as he placed them in the playpen then turned to her. He laid his hands on her hips gently. "I'll be back closer to when you close up to help with the girls, if you need me call me, okay?"

She nodded her head and before she could pull away he tilted his hat back and kissed her with the same urgency as their first kiss yesterday.

She felt the warmth spread across her body as she kissed him back.

He slowly pulled away and headed out to his truck next door.

Her heart pounded in her chest as she went to the door and locked it. That man wasn't safe to be doing these things with, only her body seemed to refuse to listen. But she had to make it listen, some way, somehow.

Eli pulled into his driveway, but something nagged at him to turn around and go back to Andie and the girls even though he knew it would probably just make her angry. Six hours, they would only be out of his sight for six hours.

What could possibly happen in six hours? Shit, his brother and Candice died in less time than that.

His hand tightened on the steering wheel as he stared at the dark, empty house. He replayed that night in his head.

Candice had Lily ready around five, she and Caleb took Lily to Andie about six, they had been dead for at least five hours before he had woken up and received the message at four a.m.

So somehow between seven and eleven p.m. they had the run in with the robber. Four hours alone, together, just loving each other and wham! Gone.

But why would someone go after Andie? Then again why would someone go up against his brother? He was bigger than Eli, more muscle, a couple inches taller. Most people in their right mind wouldn't approach men their sizes.

And yet, someone had, maybe because they had the gun. He had to get his head on straight and trust that if Andie sensed danger she'd call him and the cops. He let out another sigh and headed inside where he fixed himself more coffee then got ready for the day.

He headed out to the barn, where Dale already was.

"Hey, boss, late night?" Dale mused as his eyes crinkled and twinkled as he smiled.

"Yeah, you could say that," Eli answered as he took another chug of his coffee from the foam cup he had poured it in.

"Andie Malone finally keeping you entertained?"

"Not in the way you're thinking, she's been having some weird feelings." Eli sighed as he adjusted his Stetson and took another swig of the hot liquid in his cup.

Dale's smile turned into a serious frown. "Weird feelings? Toward you, or what?"

"Like someone's watching her and the girls, I went over yesterday and it happened again, so I stayed the night on a very small, uncomfortable couch to make sure they all stayed safe or to give the person she feels may be watching them, the hint that she's with someone and not alone, I want to tell Murphy, Carl, or Dean but you know none of them will do anything until there is proof." He let out an aggravated breath.

Dale laid a hand on his shoulder, "Why don't you have her stay here? I mean it's safe here, an alarm system, us hired hands would help out, and keep a look out for her and the girls."

Eli met his soft brown eyes. "Yeah, but she's got the bakery, that's how she makes her living and supports the girls, I doubt she'd go for it."

Dale's brown eyes twinkled a little. "She could still run it, we could find someone we know very well to watch the girls here, someone could always guard her while she's at the bakery, escort her back here and one of us could keep watch over the girls and the sitter."

Eli thought about it for a minute. "But who would watch Lil and Lucy? No one's been too helpful to Andie the last almost two years she's been here, I'm surprised she's stuck around as long as she has."

"She stayed because of Candice," Dale supplied quietly. "Belle might watch them."

"Your girl?"

"Yeah, I'll talk to her, see what she says."

"Okay, I'm going to head back there when she closes up today, you know I found that stubborn woman up on a ladder yesterday, wrapped up in her garden hose." He shook his head at the thought. "It could have ended badly if I hadn't shown up, she fell off of it."

Dale let out a whistle. "That woman is something else, you may have met your match with her."

Eli frowned at Dale a little. "What do you mean?"

"Oh, come on, everyone knew Caleb and Candice were trying to set you two up, might have been the reason they gave her custody of Lil, to bring you two together," Dale suggested.

Eli stood there silent for a few minutes, yeah Caleb had given some hints to him. But had Candice been in on it too? Had she tried to sell him on Andie and when he didn't bite it made her even more secluded? Shit. He was an ass hat.

Someone didn't kiss back like that unless they had had feelings before. He hung his head and rubbed the back of his neck. What was he going to do?

He left Dale to go start the work that needed done with so many thoughts of Andie running through his mind.

Before he knew it, it was almost ten. He rushed into the house, grabbed a change of clothes, and his body wash. Just in case he ended up staying with Andie again. He would worry about her if he didn't.

Andie let out a breath as a few more straggling customers walked into the shop and she hurried up with helping them.

She glanced at the clock, Eli said he'd be there before she closed and he wasn't. She closed her eyes briefly. She had believed him and she shouldn't have.

She could only depend on herself and that's the way it had to be. She rung up the last customers then followed them to the door. She flipped the sign when she heard the girls let out screams.

She turned around quickly, fear squeezed her heart, someone was crouched down in front of the playpen. "Excuse me, I'm closing now, I need you to leave."

He stood and turned toward her. She sucked in a sharp breath. She rushed to the girls putting herself between him and the playpen.

"Hello, beautiful, how're you?" his raspy voice raked against her skin.

"You're not supposed to be here, you can't be here." She glared at the man she thought she had loved at one time. She felt nothing as she stared into his lifeless, beady black eyes.

"Yeah, news about Candice got to me, I know how close you two were, so I figured I'd check to see how you were handling it." He stepped closer to her.

"Oh, what, now you care? Well, you see I'm fine now, so you can leave." She glared at him more.

He stepped even closer and reached out to touch her cheek but she slapped his hand away from her. "Oh, come on, Andrea. I'm sorry, I've missed you."

"Well, I haven't missed you. I'll never forget what you did, what you almost caused, you need to leave, Daryl, now." She folded her arms across her chest trying her best not to show any fear.

"Come on, love, I just want to talk, which one is mine?" he asked and went to step around her.

She hurried into his path and pushed him away from the girls. "That's none of your damn business, you'll never know either."

He reached out and gripped her cheeks painfully between his thumb and fingers. "That dirty mouth of yours always set me off. I have a right to know which one is my daughter."

She slapped his hand away from her and pushed him back again. "Over my dead body, how long have you been here?"

Daryl shrugged his shoulders as his dark gaze hardened more. "You know you're not supposed to question me."

She reached in her back pocket to grab her phone. "And

you know you're not supposed to be anywhere near us, now leave," she demanded.

He reached out and pushed her aside. "I want to know which one is mine." He made a step toward the playpen but Andie darted in front of him again and shoved him back. He glared at her. "You dare to get between me and my daughter?" He pulled his hand back and back handed her hard. "You know better than to get in my way."

The force knocked her down and she dropped her phone, it skidded across the floor.

"Maybe you needed a reminder, now, which one is mine?" he yanked her up by her hair tightly.

"Fine, neither one of them, I lost the one you put in me."

"You're a lying bitch, I will leave as soon as you tell me."

"Go to hell, asshole," she gritted out and she saw his hand raise again. She knew it was going to hurt.

"Hey! Leave her alone!" the male voice shouted from behind them.

Andie's eyes darted around Daryl. Eli. Thank God.

Daryl shoved her back to the ground as the girls started to cry.

Andie went to comfort them but was met with another slap to the face. The next thing she knew Eli and Daryl were on the ground fighting. Eli had tackled Daryl and slammed his fist into Daryl's face.

Andie scrambled to her phone and began to call 9-1-1. She explained what was going on hurriedly.

They had an officer en route and Andie grabbed both girls. She tried to soothe them as she took them away from the violence going on. Eli was giving some good punches.

Andie rushed to the kitchen with Lily and Lucy. She sat down against a bare wall and began to rock them gently, hoping the cops would show up soon.

She held the girls closer to her when she heard other voices in the shop. She fought the tears that wanted to fall. Her scalp stung a little from Daryl yanking on her hair and her face stung a lot.

"Andie?" the deep male voice called as the metal door swung open.

"Eli?" she whispered.

He rushed to them and knelt in front of her. "Are you okay?"

She nodded her head a little then he pulled all three of them into his arms.

"I'm so sorry I was late, time seemed to slip away from me, are Lil and Lucy okay?"

"I think so, a little upset but I didn't let him touch either of them."

"Was that Lucy's father?"

"More like sperm donor but, yeah, that was him." She fought the sob trying to get out.

"Carl and Dean are here, they want to talk to you." He stood and helped her up then took Lily gently. He held Lily and her and Lucy close to him as they headed out to the shop area.

Carl and Dean were standing, whispering but fell silent the minute they walked out.

Andie glanced at the two officers. And so it begins, the rumors she didn't want Eli to get caught up in. But he asked for it.

Carl stepped forward, she met his soft, deep blue eyes, they seemed sympathetic but that didn't mean he approved of Eli being around her.

"Have a seat you two," he began than sat down across from them. "Who is that man?"

"My ex, he's not supposed to be near me, restraining order," Andie answered not flinching, nor averting her gaze from Carl. "He's not supposed to be near Lucy either."

"Why?" he asked after he wrote some notes down.

"Well, obviously, because he has a short fuse and is abusive," she answered not wanting to talk about it.

"So abusive you had a restraining order put against him for Lucy as well?"

"Yes."

"And why did a judge agree to that?"

She bit the inside of her cheek as she adjusted Lucy. "Because he didn't and doesn't want kids."

"Why was he here?"

"I don't know, I haven't seen him since the day I filed the order, they kept him away from me when we had it settled in court."

"Why?"

She bit her lip hard as she glanced out the window and saw Daryl thrashing around in the cop car. "So he didn't hurt me again, they wanted him away from me during the trial. Candice made sure it was carried out," she whispered as she looked at Carl.

"Must have been pretty bad, huh?"

Andie shrugged her shoulders. "I'm still alive."

Carl narrowed his gaze at her a little.

She didn't squirm like most would have under that gaze.

"How bad was it?"

"I'm sorry, what does that have to do with today?" she asked, her voice returning to her a little more.

"We want to know how dangerous he can be. We need to know if he has ever broken the restraining order before?"

"No, then again, he's never found me before, he said he heard about Candice and wanted to make sure I was handling it okay."

"How bad was it, Andie?" Carl asked his voice softer than before.

"Bad enough I almost lost Lucy," she whispered as she pulled her daughter closer to her.

"Yet Candice and Caleb gave you guardianship over Lily, did Caleb know about the guy?"

"Y-yeah, of course he did, I stayed with them after that night, I got away as soon as I could and I came to stay with Candice and him, on Caleb's request."

Eli was tensing up beside her. "What's that got to do with any of this?"

"Seems a little odd that shortly after they were killed her ex shows up out of the blue," Dean interrupted.

Andie's eyes flew to the other man. "What are you suggesting?"

"Are you sure he didn't know where you were, that maybe you guys would plan to take off with Lily after Candice and Caleb were disposed of, then would give her back to Eli for a price?"

Eli was the one to demand an answer, "Again, what are you guys implying? I think we're done here, he broke the order, shouldn't you be giving him the third degree?"

"Well, your ranch is finally booming, great steady income, maybe her baby's daddy killed your brother and sister-in-law because she knew she would be the guardian. Boom, trade Lily for money."

Andie just stared at the two men. "Because I want every fancy thing in the world," she said sarcastically. She glanced at both cops. "I didn't know Candice and Caleb made me the custodial holder until that will was read, I love Lily as much as I love Lucy, and you want to know how bad it was?

"He kicked me repeatedly in my stomach, beat me until almost every inch of me was black and blue, he threw me down a flight of stairs. That's how bad he didn't want kids, he was trying to make me miscarry Lucy, my neighbor just by chance heard me scream and called the cops.

"The doctor thought I was barely going to make it, let alone Lucy, who I wasn't even supposed to be able to have to begin with." She glared at the men but kept her tone level so she wouldn't scare the kids.

"Okay, Andie, okay." Carl held up his hands. "We just needed to do our jobs, when Murphy heard about the call she wanted us to question you."

"Why me? And why now?"

"We still can't find anything on their murders, she was starting to think you had motive."

She felt her stomach knot up and roll, she felt like she was going to be sick. "How could I have had anything to do with it? I had Lily and Lucy from seven that night and I loved Candice, she was my only family."

"She thought up the money scandal, she's getting desperate."

Andie looked at Eli, his gaze was trained on the officers before them. He had so much anger radiating off of him, he looked almost dangerous.

"You can tell Murphy to screw off, there was a reason Candice and Caleb left Lil to Andie, so tell her I said to keep looking and back off of Andie. Is Murphy losing her edge or what?" he demanded and then pulled Andie to her feet. "Come on, baby, let's get you three home." He opened the shop door and waited for Carl and Dean to leave before he took her out of the bakery, locked it up, and led her home.

And she let him. She felt so lost and numb. Why would they think she had anything to do with Candice and Caleb's deaths?

Had they forgotten how sick she had gotten after she identified them? She let out a choking sob but pulled her emotions back in as she and Eli walked back to her house.

She hurried to the nursery and changed Lucy then traded Eli, who had followed her.

There was such a strain between them now or was it just her? Now he'd try to take Lily away and her heart broke at the thought.

They fed the girls and put them down for their naps. She expected Eli to leave but he didn't. He went to the living room while she went to take a shower. How the hell was she going to prove she had nothing to do with her best friend and her husband's deaths?

Chapter 12

Anger was filling Eli even more as he stood in front of the couch, staring out the window. He didn't want to even think about what would have happened if he had been any later than he already had been.

He dug his phone out of his pocket and made a phone call. "What the hell are you playing at? Having Carl and Dean question Andie about Caleb and Candice, you saw how shook up she was that night," he practically growled into the phone.

"I know, Eli, I'm just excluding all possibilities, she had a motive, she was going to get custody of Lily. Did you know Lucy is probably the only kid she'll ever have?"

"Oh come on, Murphy, I'm sure if she finds the right guy she'd have more kids," Eli retorted.

"No, I won't," the soft voice whispered behind him.

He turned to see Andie in a light pink tank top and black shorts. "Just take it off the table, Murphy, there's no way she did it, you may want to ask that asshole if he's been following Andie around though." He ended the call and went to put his arms around Andie but she stepped back from him.

"So, that was Murphy?" she wrapped her arms around herself tightly as she barely met his eyes.

"Yeah it was, I know you didn't have anything with Candice and Caleb."

"But she's dug into me enough to know I was told I'd never have kids, every doctor I went to while I was pregnant with Lucy was surprised I was even carrying her, let alone that she was born healthy."

"But you did it once, it's possible you could again."

Andie shook her head quickly. "No, I don't even want to try, the letdown would be too great, and no one would want to even try with me. I'd have to tell whoever wanted to be with me about it and the chances are slim to none, you proved that," she whispered and turned away from him.

Eli sighed, he had been such a jerk when his brother and her best friend had been alive and trying to push them together. That had been why there had been so many times that Caleb would strum up a conversation about Andie. They wanted him and her together. Eli pulled her back to him. "I didn't know what they were trying to do until now, Caleb and Candice were trying to push us together. Caleb always talked to me about you, when did Candice start talking about me to you?"

She looked away. "I don't know what you're talking about."

He sighed as he brushed his fingertips against the bruise on her cheek. "Are you sure you're okay?"

"Yeah," she looked up at him. "Thank you for helping."

He moved closer to her and lifted her into his arms and headed to the couch. "Do you think he's been the one giving you the weird feelings lately?"

"I don't know, I didn't feel it when he was in the shop, then again, I guess he was more focused on the kids. All I could think about was closing up and that you weren't there yet but figured you got busy."

He sat down and held her in his lap. "I didn't forget, I promise, time just went faster than normal, as soon as I realized I headed here."

She was tense in his arms. "It's okay, but you can go back to the ranch, we're fine here. I just hope you believe what you told the detective."

"Of course I do," he made her look at him. "They knew what they were doing making you Lily's mom." He hugged her small body to his. "All I would have been doing was trying to make the ranch bigger, so Lil would have everything she would have ever wanted, and she'd be with a babysitter all the time."

"I wouldn't blame you if you took her though, she was in so much danger today and I couldn't stop—"

Eli pressed his lips to hers cutting her off, he pulled back from her slowly, "She's where she's supposed to be, Andie, it's okay, I'm not taking her. Look, why don't you guys come to the ranch tonight for supper? Mom and Dad will be there, I'm sure they'd love to see the girls and you." He hated that this was going against what he had planned, he didn't want to leave his girls unprotected and here he was going to leave because it was what she wanted, even though it was going against what he suddenly wanted.

"Okay, I'll be over when the girls wake up from their naps," she whispered.

"I can stay until then."

"No, it's fine, I'm sure they'll keep him locked up for a little bit at least."

"You can stay there with me tonight. I feel better having you guys close to me for now until we figure out what's going on. Lil's room is still set up, it'd be perfect for the girls."

"I don't know, Eli, I'll have to think about it." She stood from his lap and moved across the room. "You should go."

Eli didn't want to leave, Andie's voice sounded so broken. She couldn't have kids? It seemed strange she had Lucy though. "Andie, what if we found you another doctor for a different opinion, then maybe you wouldn't shut yourself off from people so much, it could open so many more possibilities."

"Because no man would want a woman who he couldn't have more kids with? Maybe that's why they chose me, they knew I didn't have a reason to bring men in and out of Lily's life, they knew I was done because no man would ever want someone like me. I had one kid and couldn't have more, now I'll have two and can't offer more, what's the point in finding out all over again what I already know?"

"Andie, stop." He placed his hands on her shoulders but she pulled away from him.

"Just go back to the ranch, Eli. I'll be there for supper, but then I'll be coming home after."

He stepped in front of her and hugged her anyway. Then quietly left. Now things were becoming a little clearer but still didn't make complete sense.

If they knew Andie couldn't have any more children and wasn't even supposed to have Lucy, then why would they have tried to set him up with her?

He would have eventually wanted kids of his own, wouldn't he? But then he'd lose Andie, Lucy, and Lily. He didn't want that, did he? He had so much to figure out before he made another move on Andie.

He couldn't string her along and then one day decide he wanted more kids and end up leaving the ready-made family Andie held together so well. He couldn't hurt all three of them. Or would he be happy with just the three of them? Or he could talk her into maybe adopting, there was so much he had to figure out. But could he give Andie the hope she obviously had had at one point in time in him thanks to Caleb and Candice?

He ran a hand against his weary face as he got up into his truck. Fuck. What was he going to do?

Andie let out a sigh, she knew he wouldn't be the one, and yet why did it hurt so bad? It didn't even hurt this much when Daryl had turned his back on her and tried to cause the miscarriage.

She was right when she had told Candice and Caleb to stop pushing around the idea of Eli and herself. In the beginning before the wedding she had been hopeful. Who wouldn't want a man like him?

And now, they were trying to push them together all over again and she couldn't tell them to stop. But as she had told him before, she wouldn't keep Lily away from him. After tonight they'd have to come up with a visiting arrangement. And she and Lucy wouldn't be involved or hanging around anymore.

It was for the best. She had to keep that drilled into her brain and her heart.

Four-thirty finally came around. Andie gathered up the two playing babies and headed out to the car. Then she made her way to the Cameron Ranch slowly. She didn't want to do this but Maisy and Todd needed to see Lily.

Maybe she could just drop Lily off and insist she come back later. It wasn't like Eli would put up a fight to get her to stay now that he knew the truth about the non-possibility of more kids with her was in the open.

She had her precious miracle and she didn't think she wanted to jeopardize ever having another one. The doctors had to watch her so closely during the pregnancy. Especially after the attempted forced miscarriage.

She pulled up next to the blue Jeep Cherokee that was next to Eli's gray two-fifty. She let out a sigh, she'd never see that truck outside her bakery or house ever again. She closed her eyes tightly. *Just shut off all emotion, only show any toward Lily and Lucy, no one can hurt you if you are emotionless, and you are, you're cold hearted and no one gets any but your daughter and Lily, who's now your daughter also, and Candice, but she's gone.'* She ached so much but it was her own fault.

She knew she shouldn't have let Eli in and she was paying for the gigantic mistake. She opened her eyes and stared blankly ahead. Just get through this night then everything will go back to the way it was supposed to be. She let out a shaky breath then got out of the car.

She opened the back door and put the bags over her shoulder and started to get Lily. She looked up when the other door opened and Eli got Lucy. She narrowed her eyes at him but adjusted Lily and shut the door harder than necessary.

She walked around the car and went to take Lucy. "I was thinking I'd just come back for Lily later." Her tone was a little cold even to her own ears.

"Why? You're already here, and that'd be a waste of another trip back home then back out here, plus I thought you were staying here tonight."

"No, I told you I wasn't."

"Then I'm coming back with you."

"No, you're not."

He narrowed that coppery glare on her, "We already discussed I want to make sure you are safe tonight."

"And Lily will be, even if I have to stay up all night to keep her safe, I will."

"At least stay for dinner?" he almost pleaded, it was as if he genuinely wanted her to stay. But why?

"Fine, one dinner, then after this we'll set up a visiting schedule where Lily can come stay with you for a few hours or days, which ever works better." She brushed off his hand that he went to place on her shoulder and headed to the house.

———

Eli just stared after Andie for a minute. The coldness she surround herself with before was back. And in full force. God, he wanted to break it down and keep it down for good. But how? He was so uncertain of what he wanted in the future, he didn't know what to do.

They headed to the kitchen where the delicious smells of fried chicken, buttery mashed potatoes, gravy, and apple pie wafted from.

His stomach growled loudly as he followed Andie, not only with his feet but with his eyes as well. His gaze took in a lavender colored tank top that showed off her cleavage well and a pair of dark jeans with little rhinestones glued to the back pockets which glistened as the light hit them. The way those jeans hugged her bubble butt made him ache.

He let out a soft groan as he was mesmerized by the little wiggle in her walk. She'd never let him near her unless he could talk her into a couple of times. He mentally kicked himself, she wasn't that type of girl.

He tried to push everything away as they walked into the kitchen.

Maisy turned toward them. "Oh, there's my baby," she said excitedly as she stepped forward.

———

Andie moved to the side quickly as Eli took Lily from her and left her with Lucy, she let Maisy and Eli interact with Lily. She slowly moved out of the kitchen. She didn't belong there. She should have just dropped Lily off and gone back home.

She went out the front door quickly, found herself holding Lucy closer to her and made her way to the wooden porch swing.

She let out a shaky sob as Lucy laid her head against Andie's shoulder. She rubbed Lucy's back gently as she moved the swing slowly. So many nights Candice and she sat out here just looking at the stars and chatted about everything going on in life.

Her eyes began to fill with tears. She wanted her best friend, she didn't belong anywhere now. Lucy let out a squeal so Andie placed her down on the porch with a blanket and toys.

She gazed out toward the open green, low rolling hills, zoning out a little bit. "What do you think, Lucy Lu, should we go home and let this family be a family tonight?"

As Maisy took Lily from Eli he turned to talk to Andie. His stomach dropped when he didn't see her. He turned to look at his mom quickly, "I'll be right back, you got Lily pad for a minute?"

"Of course," Maisy answered as she kissed Lily and began to talk to her a little.

He rushed down the hallway that he'd just followed Andie down, checking rooms as he went. *'Where could she be?'* He headed to the front door and threw it open, his gaze landed on her and Lucy and the knot in his stomach relaxed. He leaned against the house as she placed Lucy on the porch on the blanket.

Her gray eyes looked so sad. "What do you think, Lucy Lu, should we go home and let this family be a family tonight?"

The stomach drop happened again. He rushed over to Andie and Lucy, he scooped Lucy up and sat down beside Andie. "You are family, Andie."

She looked at him, eyes a little round but still turned to steel. "I'm not, Eli, and it's okay, I get it. I don't have to be here, I can come back to get Lil later, it's not a problem."

"Well, it's a problem for me, I want you here. I want Lucy here, you two are my family now. Yeah, mainly because Candice and Caleb apparently pushed us together again but I'm fine with that, you need somewhere to belong and that is here, Andie."

She looked into his eyes, it was crazy how those eyes of hers were so shut down but expressive every time he gazed into them. He saw the pain, the loss, the need she was obviously feeling every time he looked into them.

He tilted his hat up a little and he leaned down toward her, his lips inches from hers, and said, "So, please say you'll stay for supper."

"Okay," she breathed out and his lips claimed hers gently.

But it didn't last long enough for him as Lucy let out a squeal. He pulled back from Andie and looked at Lucy, he smiled at her. "What? Do you want kisses too?" he said teasingly and pressed his lips to her cheek and kissed and nibbled making her grab his cheeks and laugh loudly.

He pulled back and stood up, cleaning up the toys and blanket, then pulled Andie from the porch swing and led her into the house.

He wrapped his arm around Andie as they walked into the kitchen. Maisy and Todd were getting the table ready with all the food while the apple pie sat on the stove to cool down. He pulled a chair out for Andie and then cursed a little.

"What's the matter, Eli?" Maisy asked as her eyes darted up to him.

"I don't have another highchair for Lucy, oh well, I'll hold her while we eat." He pulled the chair out next to Andie and sat down beside her.

Three pairs of eyes turned on him as he settled Lucy onto his lap but he didn't care. He began to place food on Andie's plate, knowing she would take less than she should.

They began to eat and the conversation stayed revolved around Lily and Lucy and how they were getting along. How Andie was managing both of the girls. Dinner was finally over and Maisy began to get the pie ready, Andie refused to eat any pie while she took Lucy back from Eli.

His gaze all through dinner kept drifting to her, he just couldn't help it. She was so beautiful. He really had to figure out what he was going to do with his life. And fast.

After the pie, Maisy and Todd decided to head home for the night. They kissed the girls, Eli, and hugged Andie.

Eli led Andie into the living room and put the girls in the playpen Candice and Caleb had set up in there. He pulled her down onto the couch slowly. "I really wish you guys would stay here tonight, please? I want to keep all three of you safe until I know for sure who's been following you around, if they find out it was Daryl and they keep him locked up I'll relax a little, it's either my place, your place, or I can stay out in the driveway all night, your choice."

She looked up at him slowly. "I guess I can, I have to go back home though, for the girls' formula, extra clothes for Lucy, and clothes for myself, and some baby food."

He looked at her feeling a little concerned. "Do you want me to go with you?"

"No, I can do it, plus the girls seem to be having fun so I don't want to interrupt them."

He let out a heavy sigh. "Okay, let me know when you get there, when you are heading back also."

"Okay, I will." She got up from the couch and he did the same.

He followed her to the door and stopped her before leaving. "Remember to let me know."

"Yes, Eli."

Before she made it out the door, he pulled her up against him gently and kissed her softly. He brushed his fingers against her cheek softly and then let her go.

He stood in the doorway until she got to her car and left the driveway. He sighed and headed back into the living room to watch the girls. He hoped everything would be okay. He had a feeling that something was just stabbing in his gut and that something wasn't right.

Chapter 13

A ndie felt disgusted with herself by giving in to Eli. But she knew she couldn't let him stay in the driveway all night and she just wanted him to leave her alone too.

She was glad she hadn't fully kissed him back on the porch swing. But the way he was with Lucy tonight made that ice barrier crack a sliver but she couldn't let that happen.

Lily would always have her Uncle Eli but she and Lucy were not meant to have him. The girls finally weren't around.

As she watched the ranch grow smaller and smaller in the rearview mirror the tears began to fall. He would make one very special woman happy and it would never be her. There was nothing special about her. Just a single mom who put everything into the bakery. Yeah nothing special.

The tears continued to fall, the pain of losing Candice, the heartbreak from the devilishly handsome, Eli Cameron, again. The stress of keeping everything together all came out in tears.

She wanted to scream, punch something, ask why and who. The way things were going the truth may never be known.

She finally made it to town and to her road. She began to

drive past the bakery and jumped when she thought she saw something. She stopped and stared at the shop as the sun was barely able to shine much light on it.

She headed to her driveway when nothing else seemed to move.

But something grated against her skin as she got out of the car and rushed to her front door. She pulled her phone out of her pocket. Her fingers and body trembled as she scrolled to Eli's number, which didn't take long since she didn't have very many people in her phone.

She got in the house and locked the door quickly, she still didn't feel safe. Eli's voice calmed her a little bit.

"Andie?"

"Eli, I think someone's at the bakery. I thought I saw something move as I drove by but I can't be sure, and the feeling is back," she quickly said into her phone as she tried to get the things she needed to go back to the ranch.

"All right, just calm down, okay? I'm on my way, call the cops, Andie, please?"

"What about the girls? I don't want them near if something is really going on, I'll call the cops too." She let out a little scream when she heard two muffled pops.

"Andie, what?"

"I don't know, I thought I heard two popping sounds."

"Where are you?"

"In the house."

"Okay, listen to me, get anything you need but don't turn any lights on, that way they don't know you're there. Stay in the house until I get there. I'll handle the girls and then I'll be there, just call 911 please?"

"O-o-okay."

"Andie, I'm serious. Wait for me in the house."

They ended the call and she dialed 911 while she did what Eli had instructed. This wasn't good at all.

As soon as Eli got off the phone he called Dale. "Dale, I need you and Belle to get here to the ranch, something's wrong at the bakery and I have Lil and Lucy."

"Okay, boss, we're on our way, we'll be there in like five."

Eli hung up, ten minutes before he could get to Andie and that time would kill him. He began to pace as he sent a text to Andie.

She didn't text him back. Fear was swimming through his veins along with anger. He should have gone with her. Why didn't he? Dale and Belle finally showed. "The girls are in the playpen in the living room, there's a little bit of baby food, snacks, and a little formula left, I'll be back as soon as I can, thank you!"

He rushed to his truck and tore out of the driveway. All he wanted was to get to Andie. Fast.

Fear gripped him harder when he pulled up to the bakery. The main light was on, and the huge window looked as if it had been busted out. He rushed to the house and walked in, he couldn't find Andie anywhere.

He knew where she was right away. Bakery.

Andie had only wanted to get away. She started gathering everything she needed to put into her car until she heard sounds of items breaking and glass smashing coming from the bakery. Someone was destroying what she had worked so hard for.

She rushed over and saw the huge window shattered, the logo of the two cupcakes and 'Andie's Sweets' was gone. There were still slivers hanging from the frame.

She heard more smashing and she rushed into the shop.

"Hey, stop it!" she yelled when she walked in and saw the black-clothed person destroying everything.

Tables were overturned, some completely broken away from their stands. And the cases were shattered. Glass was everywhere, chairs smashed. Everything she worked for, gone.

The black-clothed person came at her and grabbed her tightly. She tried to stumble away from the person but they yanked her forward and wrapped their hand around her throat.

She pulled her hand back and slammed it into their nose. She shouldn't have come in here. The guy's head snapped back but he slammed her down on the floor.

Her arm landed in the shattered glass and the person climbed on top of her. Her arm stung from the glass digging into her arm. The man began to put more pressure on her throat cutting her airway off.

She kicked and tried to get the man off of her. She was losing her ability to breathe quickly, everything was starting to fade. Her vision began to blur.

"Get money from that rich uncle of the girl you're taking care of. You owe me, bitch, then I'll leave you alone," his raspy voice gritted out.

She tried to claw against his hands on her throat but she had no strength. Her hands fell to the ground as her vision blurred and faded even more.

Then blackness.

Eli rushed into the bakery and saw the dark clothed man on top of Andie. Adrenaline washed over him and he tackled the guy off of Andie. He got a punch to the face and the man got out from under him and took off out the back as the cops pulled up.

Red and blue lights flashed against the darkness outside.

Eli crawled to Andie, tears pricked the back of his eyes as he saw her lying there limp and barely breathing. "Andie, wake up, please?" he begged her.

Andie heard the voice she was getting used to. "Eli," she rasped out.

"I'm here, Andie, right here," she felt his hand brush her hair away from her face. "I'm here."

"The girls?" she mumbled.

"They're home, sweetheart, are you okay?" he rubbed his thumb against her cheek.

She went to move but winced. "Throat hurts, my arm too."

She heard two pairs of feet pounding into the bakery. She didn't want to open her eyes, she clutched Eli's arm that was closest to her.

"Dean, Carl, we need an ambulance, she's bleeding and was unconscious for a little bit," Eli ordered. "Andie, what happened, talk to me, baby."

"He, he was trashing the place, told him to stop, he attacked me, told me to get money from Lil's rich uncle, that I owed him."

Eli slowly lifted her up into his arms and held her close rubbing her head gently, keeping her hair out of her face. She turned her face into his chest.

"I'm sorry, Eli."

"Shh, you're okay," he whispered against her ear.

"Eli, as soon as the ambulance gets here and they check her over you can take her home."

"Thanks, Carl." Eli held her a little tighter.

She heard the sirens coming down the road and she turned in to Eli more. Her arm felt so wet, the blood was starting to settle in her nose. The pain was dull but still there. Her throat was hurting too. She just wanted to go home, but she wasn't going to feel safe there.

"Are you sure the girls are okay?" she mumbled.

"Yeah, baby, they are. Hey, the ambulance is here, c'mon let's get you taken care of then I'll get you home." He pulled her up into his arms more and stood, taking her out to the ambulance.

He didn't let her go even as the paramedics pulled the glass shards from her arm. She winced at each dig of the tweezers.

They checked her throat, her breathing, bandaged her arm then sent them on their way.

Eli carried her to his truck and placed her onto the seat gently.

"I-I need to get, my things." She tried to get out of the truck.

"No, sit there, I'll get everything, where is it?"

"My car." She moaned as she leaned her head back against the headrest. She felt so weak. She just wanted to sleep. She slowly took in the sight of the front of her beloved bakery. Tears began to fall from her eyes.

Everything was gone. She let out a shaky sob as the tears fell. She was scared, angry. It would be a long road to replace everything. She should be grateful she was alive, and she was for the sake of her babies. But how much more could she handle?

The crying came harder and faster as Eli got into the truck.

"Oh, Andie, come here, baby," he whispered and moved a little closer putting his arms around her, pulling her into him. "We'll fix it, baby."

She shook her head a little bit.

"Shh, don't worry about anything right now, baby. Let's just get you safe again, for now, we'll tackle everything else later on."

She nodded her head and instead of pulling away he moved them both closer to the steering wheel, he sat in the driver's seat and she was in the middle seat. He turned the truck on, shifted gears, then wrapped his arm around her shoulders and pulled her closer to him.

He did a U-turn and headed back to the ranch.

She closed her eyes as the truck rocked gently. She didn't even know how she felt, it was just nonexistent. She never would have dreamed any of tonight would have happened but it had.

Eli rubbed her arm gently as he headed home. His intense gaze would dart to the rearview mirror as he drove. Let someone come after her or the girls, he'd shoot first and ask questions later.

He wasn't messing around anymore. He'd keep all three of them safe. No matter what. He finally pulled up to the house. He pulled his arm from around Andie, shifted the truck into park, then turned it off.

He got out and grabbed the bag he had put in the back seat, then looked back at Andie. "Come here, darlin'," he coaxed.

She scooted over to the driver's seat and he pulled her into his arms and carried her toward the house.

As he walked in he was met by Dale and Belle.

"Oh my God!" Belle screeched out a little.

Eli looked at himself and Andie. He let out a sigh, they both were covered with Andie's blood. "It's okay, Belle, we're fine for the most part."

"What the hell happened?" Dale pulled Belle against him protectively.

"She went to get things from home, the bakery was being ransacked, she tried to stop it, they attacked her."

"Oh my God, that's terrible," Belle quietly cried out.

Andie turned her head into Eli's chest trying to hide herself from them.

"Where are the girls?" Eli asked looking down at Andie.

"Asleep, they were getting so tired. Lil's in her crib and we got the play and pack set up for Lucy," Belle answered.

"Thank you guys, so much, for everything." Eli began to head down the hallway to one of the other bedrooms.

"Eli, does she want any help getting cleaned up?" Belle called making a step toward them when he turned to face Belle and Dale.

He looked down to Andie. "Darlin', do you want any help?" all he got out of her was a shoulder shrug. She was so defeated right now. He kissed her forehead. "It's up to you, she can help you, you can do it yourself, or I can help you."

"I can do it," she mumbled.

He shook his head at her stubbornness. "It's okay, Belle, she wants to do it herself, if she needs some help tomorrow, will you be free?"

"Yes, of course. Dale also talked to me about watching the girls, I'll do it if that's what you want me to do. I'd enjoy it very much, those two are so adorable." Belle smiled a small smile.

"Thanks, I'll let you know what's going on." He walked into the bedroom and sat Andie down on the bed. He heard the front door open and close. "Baby, I have to go set the alarm and get all the baby things put away in the fridge that need to be in there, then I will be right back, I promise." He kissed the top of her head gently. She was so shut down, it wasn't going to be easy to get her out of this.

He headed to the front door, locked it and armed the security alarm. He then headed to the kitchen to put the snacks, formula and baby food away. He knew how much the bakery meant to her, and it would never be the same, Candice had helped her decorate it and design it. Everything she worked hard for was stripped from her now, and her best friend couldn't even help her put it back together. He knew that's why she had shaken her head at him earlier when he said they would get it fixed. And they would, that was his promise to her. Nothing was taking her dream away from her. He hoped the cops found the man who had broken in and quickly. He was starting to think it was Lucy's dad but he just wasn't sure. He wondered if he was even still locked up.

He made a phone call as he headed to check on the girls quickly. "Murphy, you still got Daryl locked up, right?"

"Yeah, for now, he's never broken the order before so I don't know how long I can hold him, but we are looking into everything, and we're also going to do everything we can to find out who ruined 'Andie's Sweets' I promise. Where did you take her?"

"To the ranch for now, she's safer here and the girls were already here so it made sense. I don't care what it takes, Murphy, find out who did this. I am letting you know now, if it comes down to her life, or the girls' lives I will fire first."

"All right, Eli, we'll try, just keep your eyes peeled."

He ended the call and headed to the bedroom he had put Andie in. He broke into a run when he heard the scream, it sounded so ear shattering and pain stricken. He rushed into the bedroom and saw Andie pulling things off the bed one by one and throwing it across the room, screaming. He rushed up to her and wrapped his arms around her from behind as she continued to yell and cry.

He held her tightly and slowly sank down onto the floor and pulled her back against him as she continued to scream and cry. He turned her in to him a little. "Just let it out, Andie, I know, it's okay." He rocked her back and forth as she continued to cry and buried her face into his shirt and clung to it. He rubbed her back softly and just held her while she finally broke. It was gut wrenching, he almost wanted to cry for her. He never thought she would break and now she was and there wasn't anything he could do about it but let her.

She kept mumbling into his chest and cursing and yelling, the sobs shaking her whole body. She didn't deserve this to be happening, but he would let her lose it the way she had been needing to since the day she identified Candice and Caleb. His mom knew it would happen and here he was involved and there for her. He held her tighter as she clung to him more. "It's okay, baby, just let it all go," he whispered to her as they sat there on the gray carpet and he continued to rock her. They needed to get cleaned up though.

"Darlin', come on, we've got to get you cleaned up, did you bring a change of clothes and everything?" he whispered into her ear as the sobs finally subsided a little.

She nodded her head and that was it.

He let out a sigh and got up and went to the bag with her in his arms. He sat her down on the now stripped bed and got her clothes out, he saw she didn't have any bodywash or shampoo. "I have stuff you can use for a shower, I just have to run downstairs to get it," he whispered.

She grabbed his arm tightly but when he locked eyes with her she let go quickly and curled up into herself on the bed.

He let out a sigh and kissed her cheek. "I'll be right back." He hurried downstairs and got some of his things for her and headed back to her. He then scooped her up slowly and went to the hallway bathroom. He sat her down on the counter top and started the water. "Are you sure you're going to be able to do this by yourself?"

She shrugged her shoulders. He closed his eyes and bit the inside of his cheek. This was going to be so rough on her. He just needed to give her time, she'd come back around. He turned the water on, left to check on the girls again then grabbed the monitor and put it in the bathroom with them. He felt the water and it felt warm enough.

"It's ready, Andie."

"Okay," she whispered but just sat there on the counter.

He was going to regret this, he hung his head a little as he took his Stetson off and walked in front of her. His eyes landed on the bruises around her throat, his fingers slowly trailed them, "How bad does it hurt?" he whispered.

She looked up at him. "I'm fine, Eli, it doesn't hurt, too bad, I guess."

He walked closer and pulled her down off the counter, he began to take her tank top off slowly giving her enough time to say no but it never came. He unbuttoned her jeans and the next thing he knew she was undoing his buttoned-down gray shirt. He swallowed hard and her slim fingers brushed against his hot, hardened skin. He locked eyes with her as she pushed his shirt off of him and it fell to the floor.

"Andie," he warned.

"Please?" she whispered.

He grimaced a little, he had no idea what was going on inside that spectacular brain of hers right now and he didn't want her to regret anything in the morning, but he also had the feeling she really needed help by the way she winced when she moved her arm.

He finished pushing her jeans off of her after he stripped her of her shoes and he kicked off his worn boots. "Turn around," he whispered. She did and he began to unclasp her lacy black bra. Their eyes locked in the mirror, her eyes were so round with fear, she looked so fragile, he had never seen her like this in the two years he had known her. His eyes flicked to her now free breasts, they looked so beautiful and tempting. He felt his body reacting already and he hadn't even touched her nor she him for the most part. The slightest touch from her and his body would be flamed to attention with an ache and burn, and he knew only she could quench the burn.

His hands moved to take her lacy panties off as well and his hands cupped her ass gently then he ran them up her back to her shoulders and squeezed them. His lips found the curve between her neck and shoulder. He pressed very soft kisses there and she turned toward him and looked up at him.

He moved back from her not sure what she wanted. He found out quickly as she undid his jeans and pushed both those and his boxers down. She pulled him toward the shower and she got in. He had to keep his wits about him, he couldn't do this with her after what happened. She was so vulnerable. It would only be him washing her and nothing else. It had to be that way.

He grabbed the body wash and shampoo before he stepped into the shower as well and he watched as the water flowed down her body. She was so tempting. But he wanted to do this the right way. He had to figure out where he stood in his life if he was going to be able to give her any kind of life. He slowly washed her body and her hair, then rinsed her off being careful of the bandage wrapped around her deep cuts from the glass.

He stepped back. "Why don't you get out and get dried off, if you need help getting dressed I will help you as soon as I am done in here."

She nodded her head as his eyes raked over her glistening body. It hurt so bad that he couldn't do anything about the tightening of his member as they switched places and her soft body brushed against his hard one.

He bit his lip hard trying to let her exit the shower without pulling her back and having his way with her. He rushed to get washed up and stepped out of the shower. He watched her dry off and if it was even possible he felt himself strain even more. He took a deep breath trying to muster some kind of control over himself.

As soon as he was dried off, he wrapped the towel around his waist and she had hers wrapped around her. He took her back to the bedroom where he slowly got everything cleaned up. He helped her dress in another tank top and a pair of shorts. His arousal was making a very prominent tent against the towel he had on.

"If you need anything tonight call me, Andie, I'm going to head downstairs, get some rest, baby." He kissed her cheek gently then covered her up with the blanket as she lay down. He hoped she would be okay by herself. He was so worried about her but knew he had to keep his distance until he figured out what he wanted.

She let him leave without a fight. Her tiny body looked so defeated. He wanted to pulverize the man who had hurt her and he hoped he'd get his chance to beat the guy.

Andie watched Eli leave. She didn't know what really came over her in the bathroom or what she had been begging for but she was glad he didn't do anything. She wouldn't have had the stamina or ounce of dignity to stop him tonight. She let out a shaky sob as the tears began to form again as she curled up into the firm pillow and pulled the gray cover around her tightly.

All she really wanted was to be held but this was something else she was going to have to handle on her own. She didn't need help to get the bakery fixed, she could do it herself. She'd call her insurance agent tomorrow and start to get things replaced as soon as possible. She was going to have to go tomorrow and clean it up, but she didn't know how she was going to feel okay to do it herself.

But she had to. And she hoped Eli would let her clean it up and get that woman to hopefully watch the girls like she offered because there was no way she was taking the girls into town for a while and if Eli trusted her then she supposed she could trust the woman too.

She slowly cried herself to sleep not knowing what else to do. She had finally been pushed to her breaking point and he saw it. This wasn't how things were supposed to go and now he would never even dream of being with her after that break down.

Chapter 14

Eli hated himself for running away but he didn't know what else to do to get his raging hormones under control. The poor woman was attacked tonight for crying out loud and he still acted like a hormonal teenager.

He wanted to be on that bed with her and dive into her sweetness but she needed rest. He went to the bathroom to get their bloody clothes. When he picked up her jeans, they felt heavy. He cursed when he pulled out her phone.

He took the clothes to the laundry room and headed back to the bathroom where he grabbed the baby monitor. He'd take care of the girls tonight if they needed anything.

He then made his way to Candice and Caleb's room. He had his hand around the door knob. He hadn't been in there since his parents and the Howells had gone through everything. He took a deep breath preparing himself for the plunge of cold, emptiness that was about to engulf him. He slowly walked in as he opened the door and felt how barren the room was. He missed so much, the laughter he and Caleb had, the playful banter, the fights from when they were kids. He missed it all. He headed to the dresser and found a pair of gray sweatpants.

He got them on quickly, maybe that was why he was latching onto Andie so bad, she made him feel alive. She made him feel like he was still himself even without his older brother. She made the pain ease a little bit, he just wanted to make her feel the same way eventually. He headed back to Andie with her phone in hand, he checked the charge and it was at eighty percent, better than nothing.

Before he could reach the door of the guest bedroom she was staying in, he heard the loud scream. He rushed into the room. "Andie!" he said as he saw her sitting up in the bed, trembling, and crying again. "Andie…" He laid her phone and the monitor on the bedside table then crawled onto the bed. "What happened?"

She moved away from him a little bit. "Bad dream," she mumbled as the tears fell and she stared at her hands.

He let out a breath, this was going to be a long, ache filled night. "Come here, baby."

She stared at him for a minute but didn't move.

He moved the comforter and sheet so he could lay down then he pulled her soft body against him. Her head landed against his chest softly and he stroked her back gently. "Get some sleep, baby, I'll be here the rest of the night," he whispered.

He felt her move even closer to him, he hated not knowing what else to do. But if she felt safe now then that was all he could hope for. Her body began to relax as she snuggled against him and the blanket.

He squeezed her a little. "It's okay, I'm not going anywhere, I'll be here until the morning."

"Okay," she whispered. "I'm sorry."

"You're fine, even a spitfire needs comforting." He smiled

when he heard her start to snore and her leg drifted over his a little bit.

He began to fall asleep too.

Eli let out a groan when he felt someone pushing against his chest.

"Eli, Lucy is crying, I need you to let me go." The soft voice fell across his ears as she pushed back against him more.

He opened his eyes to find Andie was more on top of him then beside him, "I'll get her," he grumbled a little. He rolled so Andie was on her back and he was nestled between her thighs. He leaned down and kissed her gently. "I'll be back, you stay here and rest." He rolled away from her and headed to the nursery. All he could really think about was how much it pained him to move away from Andie, he couldn't believe she had been on top of him like that though. He never would have expected that from her.

"Hey, beautiful girl, what's the matter?" he leaned over the play and pack and scooped Lucy up carefully. She nuzzled her face against his bare chest. "Like mother like daughter, huh?" he rubbed her back as he bounced her up and down.

He took her to the changing table and changed her diaper then scooped her tiny body back up to him. She quieted a little more as she laid her head on his shoulder.

He bounced her a little bit more. "Do you need anything else, princess?" he asked, as he rubbed her back she began to fall asleep again. "Goodnight, princess, see you in the morning."

He laid her down in the crib instead of the play and pack, then Lily began to wake up. He got her changed then she went back to sleep also. "Goodnight, Lily pad." He kissed her forehead and laid her back in the crib.

He made sure they were both content before he headed back to Andie. He laughed a little when he saw her lying in the middle of the bed. He shook his head as he climbed onto the bed, he leaned over Andie with his hands on either side of her head, "What're you doing?"

"Trying to sleep," she mumbled but opened her eyes.

He looked into them then glanced at her lips. "What were you doing on top of me?" he teased.

"That was all you, when I tried to move to get Lucy you pulled me down right on top of you," she whispered. Her voice was a little hoarse but it still sounded so sexy.

"Oh yeah?" he arched an eyebrow at her.

"Yeah, why would I lie?"

"I don't know, so I don't think you really want me." He teased as he leaned down a little.

"I don't want you, Eli."

"You are a bad liar." He leaned further down but instead of kissing her lips he went for her neck instead which caused her to arch up into him. "See, you do want me," he whispered against her ear.

"That's what happens when a woman hasn't been with a man for almost two years, at least," she gasped out as he nibbled on her ear.

"We could rectify that issue," he stupidly offered, of course, she would shoot him down at least he hoped she would for right now.

"Wouldn't that make me seem a little desperate?"

"How?" His nose trailed against her jaw line right before his lips brushed against hers.

"Sleeping with you so soon, even though we know it would only be the once."

"Maybe you couldn't resist it being just once, never know until we find out." He kissed her a little harder. He was an ass hat, she was just hurt, sure they got some sleep but his subconscious was obviously trying to tell him something if he was pulling her on top of him when she tried to leave.

He wanted to see where all of this could possibly go between them. Who cared if she couldn't have any more kids or didn't want to try? He couldn't lose this kind of banter or tension between them that promised to be good.

He kissed her deeply and she slid her tongue into his mouth, letting him drink in the sugary taste of her mouth, that was her taste alone.

***

Andie didn't know what had gotten into her, all she could feel was the same wave of want and need flood over her suddenly. She'd gained so much more respect for Eli when all he did was help her get cleaned up in the bathroom and then he'd gotten up with the girls.

She dug her fingers into his messy light blond hair with sandy highlights. It felt so thick and soft against her fingers.

The warmth spread over her like a fire. Could she give herself to this man for a moment and still be left whole again after? The logical answer was hell no, but why bother with logic when nothing lately was logical? She gasped and whimpered in protest when he pulled away but he went back to her neck.

"Andie, are you sure?" he asked between each kiss he pressed along her neck as he moved further down.

"Eli, please, make me forget what's happened in the last few weeks. Please, I want you," she answered huskily.

Screw the consequences and regrets she may have after, but right now him being on top of her, kissing her, and stirring the burn deep within her felt so right.

She was a bad liar though, she had wanted him even before the big wedding day. And every day after that, she just never wanted to bring to attention what she wouldn't be able to give him, if things didn't work out between them then she'd just do what she did before. Stay secluded, still steal the secret glances whenever she saw him in town or at the bakery.

She desperately wanted to know what being with Eli Cameron was like, even if it was temporary. She moaned when his thumb and forefinger tweaked one of her already hardening nipples, making it rise to more attention.

She felt him gather her up against him then roll to his back. She gazed down at him. Even in the softly lit room she could see those coppery eyes of his darken with desire as she fit snuggly against his strained arousal.

"You know I'm okay with waiting, I think I've proved my point and shown quite a bit also."

She heard him let out a long, harsh groan as she nudged her aching center against his hard shaft that was nested against her.

She leaned down and pressed her lips against his. He plunged his tongue in and out of her mouth, curling and dancing with her tongue then retreated but would dart in again.

She gripped the pillow below his head as heat pooled inside of her wishing he was making the same movement with his straining member inside of her.

His hands ran up her sides and cupped her breasts through her tank top. His thumbs grazed over the hard peaks. She whimpered wanting to feel his rough, calloused hands on her bare skin. It was like he knew what she wanted. His fingers pulled the top down below her breasts and his hands touched her and played with them.

He broke the kiss slowly and moved down beneath her body and caught first one rigid nipple in his mouth then the other. He rolled her over to her back. He broke the contact and pulled the tank top over her head being careful of her arm. He trailed his fingers and lips down her stomach coming to her shorts. He slowly pulled them down and kissed her leg as he made his way back up to look at her.

She blushed and went to hide herself when his gaze raked over her slowly. Like she was a meal he was going to devour. There were a few spots she hadn't lost from having Lucy, which included the C-section scar and stretch marks.

He caught her hands, pinning them above her head with one of his hands. "You're so beautiful," he rasped out. "Don't ever, ever hide when we're together like this." He kissed her softly.

All her inhibitions rushed away and were replaced with need. Her hands reached for the waist band of his sweatpants. He helped her push them down. She arched into him when she felt his prominent shaft brush against her.

He pulled her legs around his waist and slowly worked his way into her. She moaned a little at the pressure of being stretched by his fullness before he slowed down. "Sorry, beautiful." Once he buried himself to the hilt inside of her he stopped and gave her time to adjust to him. "Just let me know when you're okay," he whispered and began the torment of her lips, breasts, and neck again.

She began to rock beneath him a little. "Yes," she moaned and he began to move against her creating a friction against her aching center and sensitive jewel. The pressure built inside of her quickly and she knew it wouldn't be long before she lost herself in him.

She had never felt this kind of stretching and pleasure before. She tightened her legs around his waist as he began to nibble on her ear, sending goosebumps skittering across her skin. Then he pressed gentle kisses along her neck, the scruff from his unshaven face sending more tingles along her skin.

She dug her fingers into his hair. "Eli," she begged, for what she didn't know.

He rolled them over so he was on his back and she sunk lower into his lap. She moaned as she began to move up and down his length as he cupped her ass in his hands meeting her thrust for thrust. She let out a scream as her world shattered in a fantastic way. Thousands of colors and feelings seemed to explode around her as she clamped down around Eli's bulging shaft and he thrust up into her a few more times before he let out a loud masculine growl as he exploded inside of her.

He pulled her down to him as their ragged breathing was all that surrounded them. He began to rub his fingertips against her lower back as their breathing went back to normal.

Eli smiled when Andie snuggled into his chest, she felt so warm instead of the cold he had been feeling radiating from her. That moment was beyond earth shattering, he never thought it would be that amazing.

She was so expressive and he loved it. He kissed her forehead gently as she began to fall asleep in his arms. He adjusted her so he wasn't inside her anymore but kept her on top of him. He rubbed her back again and sighed. Yeah this was where he wanted to be forever. Who cared if they didn't have a child together, he was falling in love with his niece's guardian. Two years too late but it finally happened.

Now to make her understand he was serious. Let the hard work begin. He began to fall asleep holding Andie close to himself.

Chapter 15

Andie jerked awake as the silence around her was shattered with a louder pop than the night before. She felt the scream bubbling up inside her as she scurried out of the bed, not realizing she was wrapped up in the sheet and tumbled to the ground landing on her injured arm with a loud thud.

That made her let out the yell that was bubbling but it was more from pain this time. She heard the door open quickly and Eli was beside her in an instant. He knelt beside her and cupped her cheek. "Hey, what happened?"

"You didn't hear a loud pop?" she asked as she looked around frantically.

"Hey, no, it's okay, it was just a dream, darlin'," he assured then helped her up and wrapped the sheet around her carefully. "Did you fall on your arm?" he asked when he glanced to the bandage wrapped around her arm.

She nodded her head a little.

"Are you okay?" he asked as he sat her down on the bed.

She shrugged her shoulders. "Where are the girls?"

"Still sleeping, actually, I was getting ready to get them

when I heard you," he answered in a soft, soothing tone.

She looked up at him, she felt the heat enter her cheeks as she remembered the mind-blowing moment she had had with him the night before. Apparently it wasn't affecting him. He looked a little calm but also really tired. She looked away from him quickly. "Let me get dressed, I'll get them, Eli."

He tilted her face up gently by her chin. "I can help, baby."

She looked at him for a minute. "Why?" she said, then swallowed hard and tried to clear the sleep out of her voice. "Why do you keep calling me baby? Ever since our first kiss, I mean I've never had anyone call me it before, so I don't know."

He crouched down in front of her and locked eyes with her, they were less coppery and more golden. "Because, honestly, I don't know, I do know I like calling you it."

She searched his eyes slowly trying to read what he was really thinking. But who was she kidding, she never knew anyone as well as she had Candice. She let out a soft sigh. "Let me shower, and I'll get the girls up. I suppose you're confining me to the house today?"

It was his turn to let out a sigh, he reached up and brushed his fingertips against the bruises around the front of her throat. "I'd prefer you stayed here today, yes, it would make me feel better. There's something else I want to talk about as well. Do you remember the last thing I said to you when you called me from your house last night?"

"I-I think so…"

"Andie…" he said sternly.

"Okay, yes. I remember," she quickly responded.

"What did I say?"

"To wait for you."

"Lucky for you, I think you're too hurt to take to task. Otherwise another part of you would be extremely sore every time you sat down today," he said matter-of-factly.

"You wouldn't," she gasped.

"I would," he affirmed. "So you'll stay in the house today without complaint, right?

She nodded her head, she wasn't ready to be alone and there was no need to add fuel to the fire. "Who knows when I'll be able to clean up the bakery anyway."

"Can you do me a favor though once the girls are fed and playing?"

"Sure," she whispered wishing she could kiss those lips that had been pressed to her in so many places last night.

"Can you write down anyone in your past who has ever wanted to hurt you or needs money?"

"Honestly, besides Daryl I can't think of anyone."

"Just try once you've woken up some, there's coffee in the kitchen. If you need me call me, just try to take it a little easy, if you find you need help, call me also, and I'll have Belle come over, the girl from last night."

"Okay," she whispered and turned her gaze from him. She let out a startled gasp when he laid her back on the bed and leaned over her and pressed those lips she had been fantasizing about short minutes before, to hers with an urgency she completely felt, she ran her fingers through his thick, soft hair as she pulled him closer. Why couldn't she shut these feelings off?

He slowly pulled back from her, his breath just as hitched as her own. He pecked her lips. "I better head out before Dale gives me hell for being late, be a good girl today."

She rolled her eyes a little. "I promise. But aren't you kind of the boss?" she asked as he helped her sit up.

He winked at her. "All the more reason not to be late, I'll come check on you around lunch time."

"Okay, oh and Eli?" she called out as he headed to the door, he turned back to her a little. "I'm sorry for not listening last night. Be careful today, he might know I'm here, whoever *he* is, and I promise I'll try to figure out who he could be."

"I'll keep an eye out, I promise, I'll set the security alarm here as well."

"Thank you, Eli, for everything."

"Hope that *everything* doesn't include last night because I'm not done with you yet, by far." He smiled wickedly and out the door he went.

She swore she stopped breathing, he wasn't done with her? What on earth. She felt her face heat up and she grabbed her clothes and sighed. She was going to have to get more, her clothes from last night were no doubt probably ruined.

She'd have to have Eli take her to get things later. She bit her bottom lip and grabbed her phone and shot him a text. *If I'm staying here longer, I'll need to get more clothes, I only grabbed enough for last night and today, and Lucy will need some other things and I have to get more baby food and formula.* She sent it then went to get in the shower.

She managed a shower for the most part and dressed. She opted for no bra since she wasn't going to be going anywhere for a while. She went to get the girls, got them changed, then headed to the kitchen. She placed Lily in the highchair and fastened her in.

She sat Lucy down beside the chair for a minute then began to get everything ready. She then remembered the saucer Lily had. She scooped Lucy up and went to get it from the living room and brought it back to the kitchen. Her arm was still hurting her a little bit but it could be worse.

She put Lucy in the saucer and began to finish everything up, then fed the girls. She gave Lucy and Lily their bottles and took them to the living room. She put them in the playpen, a smile touched her lips as they began to play.

She went to the coffee table in the middle of the living room, she opened the drawer where she found a note pad and pen. She sat down facing the girls and began to rack her brain.

Who could feel like she owed them something? Particularly

money. The only people she had any interaction with was Candice, her parents, and Daryl. At age three was when she was put into the system. She never really knew what happened to her real parents. But from age three until she was sixteen she'd been placed in at least twenty-three different foster homes. No one had wanted her. Until age ten, but when the adoption was so close the sweet couple had died in a car crash.

She shivered, bad luck was just what she had, why hadn't it been her instead of Caleb and Candice? That was her kind of luck, not theirs. She had found someone else, another couple, at age fourteen, they were a little bit older, but hell what did that matter? Unfortunately, it did matter, their fostering licenses expired while she was there and they weren't able to renew them.

She wrote down fifteen last names. Those were all she could remember with being in at least twenty-three foster homes before the last one.

The man, Tame Campbell, and his wife Stella Campbell, had been the worse foster home she had been placed in, by far. Andie closed her eyes tightly. She'd almost put that last night behind her. Could that be a reason why the man would come after her?

She looked over at Lucy and Lily who were babbling away. She smiled, she would swear those two had their own little conversations. They reminded her so much of Candice and herself. Those two would be the best of friends, hopefully. They loved each other so much.

She glanced back at the notepad when all of a sudden the security alarm went off. It blared through the house as the girls broke into tears at the sound.

Geez, that was a little loud. She got up to get the girls as the fear settled in. She tripped over the table in her hurry to get to the girls when her phone began to ring. She answered as she crawled over to the girls.

"Andie, are you okay?"

"Eli, hello? I can't really hear you, it's too loud here, I don't know what's going on!" she yelled into the phone.

"Just hang on, we're on our way!" he yelled back and she caught most of what he said. She laid her phone down to try to comfort the girls.

Nothing was working, the alarm was hurting all of their ears.

Eli yelled to Dale, and one of the other hands, Levi, to check all around the house when they got to it. He should have made sure someone stayed with Andie and the girls. He thought they would be safe, he was so wrong.

He kicked his horse, Lightning, and it sent him into a gallop to the house. They were out in the farthest pasture, repairing a downed fence when he heard the alarm go off from the house. He was glad it carried to almost anywhere on the property.

He made it to the house and jumped off Lightning, dug his keys out of his pocket then bolted into the house. He silenced the alarm quickly, then headed to the crying that was coming from the living room. He saw Andie struggling with the girls, he scooped Lucy into his arms and began to calm her down as Andie managed Lily.

He pulled Andie against him. "What happened?"

"I don't know," he felt her body tremble against him. "We were out here, everything was fine until the alarm started blaring." She laid her head against him and shook a little more.

"Okay, let's go to the girls' room, I'll make sure it's safe before I leave you there, I'm going to check the house to make sure everything really is okay, I've got Dale and Levi checking the outside." He bent down to pick up her phone and slid it into her sweatpants pocket. He took them down the hall to the nursery.

He scoped out the room and closet before checking out the rest of the house. He looked everywhere on the first floor. The front door had been locked when he got there, the deck door and the kitchen were secure too. No one seemed to be upstairs. He searched everywhere and found nothing so he headed down to his domain, the basement. He checked everything down there and it all looked good. He texted Dale asking if everything was good outside.

As he waited for the reply he headed back upstairs to Andie. She was shaken up but again managing to put Lucy and Lily ahead of herself. He walked into the nursery and locked the door just in case, he sat down beside Andie as Lucy and Lily played.

He watched the girls closely but pulled Andie into his lap. "Are you sure you're okay?"

"Might be a little deaf now but other than that yeah, I guess so."

He shook his head. "Sorry about that, I wanted to be able to hear it no matter where I was out there and I'm a heavy sleeper."

She laid her head on his shoulder, as she held onto her hurt arm again. "Trust me, I kind of figured that out for myself last night, took me forever to get you to wake up so I could take care of Lucy."

He glanced at the bandage. "It's bleeding again?"

"Yeah, I tried to rush to get the girls and instead I managed to trip over the coffee table."

"First, the ladder, then Daryl, next the bakery, and now a coffee table? I'm starting to think I'm going to have to place you in a big ol' bubble so you're always safe."

She leaned back and shoved his hat over his eyes. "You were part of the ladder incident buddy and if you weren't so deaf you wouldn't have needed the alarm so doggone loud, so we're two for two. Daryl and the bakery were actually my fault."

He tilted his hat back up with a smile on his face. "Actually we're two for four, almost forgot about you toppling off backward from your car when you were fighting the spark plug wires, and you fell out of bed this morning, so I think we're going to have to invest in that bubble."

She attempted to scowl at him. "Ha, so you admit that my falling off the ladder was your fault."

"Eh, probably would have happened even if I hadn't shown up, but I'm very glad I did," he teased. When Andie opened her mouth to protest, he slid his mouth down over hers and she automatically let out a moan and relaxed in his arms.

He slowly pulled back and just held her, waiting to hear from Dale. He tensed when he felt his phone go off finally. He adjusted Andie a little and pulled his phone out but settled her right back to where she had been before. She snuggled into him as the girls crawled over to them. He leaned back against the wall as he read his text from Dale.

No sign of anything, boss, nothing out in the barns either, Levi's taking care of Lightning, we think you should stay with Andie and the girls, we got things covered out here.

He quickly sent a text to respond. *Good plan, I want to anyway. I'll need Belle a little later since Andie and the girls being here is going to last a little bit longer than we initially thought, thanks Dale. I appreciate everything.* He placed his phone on a low volume setting then laid it on the floor beside him as Lily and Lucy climbed up onto Andie.

He chuckled and kissed each of little girls' cheek then pressed his lips to Andie's as he wrapped his arms around his three girls.

Lucy snuggled into his chest as Lily did the same with Andie. The scare of the alarm apparently forgotten. He just hoped it didn't happen again. They were supposed to be safe with him. He laid his cheek against Andie's head as he began to slowly rock all three of them.

He smiled when it didn't take long for Lucy and Lily to fall asleep. Andie slowly fell to sleep too. He leaned his head back against the wall.

He had to get them safe and he didn't know how. But he'd do whatever it took. They were all his family now, all his girls and he'd never be able to walk away from them. Andie was his one, if only he had realized it sooner.

Everyone was asleep, so it was an opportunity to talk to his brother. *Thanks, big bro, you and Candice knew what I was too blind to see, sucks you're gone now but thank you for the second chance to see she's my one, just like Candice was yours.* Now he knew how Caleb felt the minute his eyes landed on Candice. If only he hadn't been so stubborn, this might be a little easier for Andie to see. *'Please help me make her see, Caleb, I need her now, once isn't going to be enough, I want all of this every day for the rest of our lives.'*

"Eli!" Andie shouted as she jerked awake, she felt an arm tighten around her. Fear gripped her heart tightly and her body tensed.

"Easy, baby, I've got you, it's okay," the deep rumble of a voice she was getting used to reassured her.

She looked up into those golden-coppery tinted eyes of his, they were darker around the edges and lighter toward his pupils. But there wasn't hardness in them. Just the same look of pure want that was a recurring feeling she'd been having ever since their first kiss. She just stared at him until she felt Lily move against her chest. She looked down at the baby snuggled against her, surprised her outburst didn't wake the little girl.

She couldn't say the same about Lucy. She stirred against Eli pressing her feet into Andie.

Eli adjusted her a little and looked back at Andie.

She let out a ragged breath she'd been apparently holding. "You let us fall asleep on you? What about the work you have to do outside?" She went to move but he held her still.

"Dale and I decided I was going to stay in here with you three. I didn't want to leave after the fiasco earlier, were you dreaming again?" he spoke softly so he didn't wake Lily up.

"Yeah, I was, it wasn't good," she whispered as she looked down to her daughters. This was becoming such a nightmare. She just wanted them to be safe and she wanted to have her normal life back, then again would it ever be normal again?

"What was it, darlin'?" he drawled in the southern tone of his that sent shivers and goosebumps along her skin.

"They got to you, whoever is doing this to me, got to you and they weren't going to let you go, because you were getting in the way of getting to me." She almost sobbed out. She had to admit she didn't want anything to happen to Eli, at some point, maybe the way he had spun her around that makeshift dance floor at Candice and Caleb's wedding, maybe the way he had changed toward her over the past few weeks, or maybe the way he had kissed her after he stopped her from getting hurt when she fell off that ladder. Or maybe it was when he'd rushed to help her at the bakery both times she'd needed him, or even last night. She didn't know exactly when it happened but she cared about Eli, not the way she had cared about Candice or the girls, but a way a woman could care for a man when she was in love. Yeah she was lost to this man and she was pretty sure it happened with just that one stupid dance.

"That won't happen, they won't get to me, and yeah I am in the way, and I'll always be in the way, have to protect the mother of my niece," he said gently as Lily began to stir and she slowly pushed up from Andie and Lucy let out a squeal of joy at the sight of her friend.

"But, what happens if something does happen to you?" Andie mumbled as she watched the girls. Eli, Lucy, and Lily were all she had left and she couldn't bear for something to happen to him or her girls.

"Nothing will happen to me, not from this asshole trying to prey on you. I'll shoot him first before anything else would happen to you or the girls or myself, okay?"

She looked up at him, he didn't have an ounce of worry about him and yet it wasn't satisfying to her. They had to find out who was doing this and quick because they both had lives to get back to and if that didn't include each other for long term then she would just have to accept that but she still didn't want to be alone again.

But that's going to happen eventually, you love the man, who's to say he loves you back? He wouldn't be holding all three of us while we slept if he didn't have some ounce of feelings for all of us, not just Lily, would he? Then again, might just be a lust kind of thing, excitement that he couldn't knock you up, so why not have fun for a little bit until he was finally ready to settle down and have a family? Her thoughts were running wild. Time to lock the uncertainty down for a while.

"Andie, you're going to have pretty bad permanent frown lines if you don't stop thinking so hard," he teased, leaned down and caught her lips briefly as his phone began to ding. He groaned a little as he adjusted Lucy so Andie could hold her too and he grabbed his phone from the floor beside him. He read the message, out loud, "Dale wants to know if we're ready for Belle to come over, she's going to watch the girls while we go pick up some more things for you and the girls to bring back here.

"Sure, will there be enough time to get the girls fed?"

"I think so," he answered as she moved from his lap carefully with having both girls but he stood and took Lucy and helped her up. "I'll help you feed them."

She turned her eyes up to him and she was pretty sure she was looking at him with the love she felt for him. It may just be heat, attraction, and lust with him but with her she was so far gone and knew there would never be another man for her. He was who she wanted, but would he want her for just as long? So many things were going through her mind as they headed down to the kitchen and she placed Lily in the highchair and Eli held Lucy. "I used that saucer today for her earlier, she didn't seem to mind, so we can use it again. If we have time I can bring her highchair out, I just don't want to bring too much though, in case this stuff gets settled soon."

"Bring whatever you want, Andie, this is your home now, so you guys deserve anything you would have in your normal home."

"Okay." She got things ready and headed back over to Eli and the babies. She let out a gasp when, instead of letting her pull out a chair, he pulled her down onto his lap. She looked at him and could feel the heat against her cheeks and the deep ache lower between her thighs. Yeah last night wasn't enough. She wanted him again. Why did she ever give into temptation? She let out a breath as he began to feed Lucy and she began to feed Lily.

"So, did you come up with a list?"

"Yeah, I did, it's out on the table in the living room, it's probably longer than you expected but also not the most accurate since I can't remember before age eight."

"Why do you say that?"

"I was bounced around from foster home to foster home most of my life since I was three, no one really stuck until I was at least eight."

"And what happened after you were eight?"

"No one wanted me, except for two of the foster parents, they were the only decent ones I was ever sent to live with."

"What happened with them?"

She let out a shaky breath as she slid the spoon into the baby food and gave it to Lily to eat. "The first ones I was with from the time I turned nine to a little after I turned ten wanted to adopt me, but they were killed in a car crash. I bounced around again then another couple got me when I just turned twelve, they were denied because of their age and their license to be foster parents needed renewed and they couldn't get that done because of their age also, it's so fucked up how the system works sometimes."

Eli rubbed her back gently before he fed Lucy another spoonful of baby food. "What happened after you were twelve?"

She glanced at him, he actually sounded like he wanted to know, he wasn't looking at her like she was downright trash either, did miracles somewhat exist? She cleared her throat, "Bounced around again, until I turned sixteen but then I ran away from that foster home because I knew I could take care of myself and anything would be better than living in that wretched place."

He stared at her intently, "How many foster homes did you stay in?"

"At least twenty, I don't remember from age three until I turned eight, but it started when I was three."

"What happened to your parents?"

"No one knows, I was found with a note wandering around the streets when I was three. I kept the note for a while, but then got rid of it because I figured it was useless, I'd never find my parents, all it said was my name and that I needed a good home, like I was a pet instead of a child." She shivered at the thought that that was what her parents had thought of her.

His gaze never left her as she talked but he still managed to feed Lucy. *Huh, a man that could multitask, who'd of thought.* She flicked her gaze to him then looked away. Maybe he was realizing she wasn't worth his time anymore.

"So, you've never really known what being loved by a parent felt like? Is that why Candice and Caleb chose you? Because you know what not to do?"

"It's possible, but honestly, Eli, your guess is as good as mine as to why they picked me, could have just been because I picked them to be Lucy's godparents. I had no one else, and I have no one else now, well except you for Lily, but I don't know what will happen to Lucy if something ever did happen to me, and now I realize last night was very fucking stupid of me. I just saw everything Candice and I had done for that shop going down the drain and it wasn't fair that that bastard thought he could do it. I should have done what you told me and waited for you at the house. I'm sorry. I was wrong."

"I'm happy to hear you apologize. Given the circumstances and now your acceptance of your mistake, I won't punish you this time. Don't think I will always do this, Andie, because I won't. There will be consequences, spanking being the least of those. I am a dominant man and plan on being the head of my household, and I expect the woman in my life to obey me. Do you understand and agree, Andie? I will never strike or hit you in anger ever. If I'm angry, I will wait until I have calmed down considerably. My intent is to help you not get yourself hurt or to risk your safety. The girls and I need you," he said with his heart on his sleeve.

"I know about the head of household lifestyle. I read a lot of books about it. And I know in my heart you would never intentionally hurt me or the girls. I trust you completely, Eli. Truly. I also know you will do your best to take care of me and the girls and I couldn't be happier or feel as safe with anyone else," she said with tears in her eyes.

"I'm certain this is the start of something special, Andie.

You and the girls are what have been missing from my life. You are mine, baby, don't forget it. Don't worry about the bakery either, I'll get it fixed up. I know it's not going to be the same, or feel the same but everything can be replaced, but you can't, so yeah no more stupid ideas like last night, okay?" he asked and she nodded her head to agree and he began again. "So, what happened with the other foster homes?"

"Same thing, no one wanted me, I'll never know why either. I always tried to behave, but sometimes my mouth got me into more trouble than anything else, if they did something I didn't like I told them, then I'd be the ungrateful child under their roof so they just kept placing me and placing me. Until I turned sixteen and landed in the last foster home." She stopped talking as they fed the girls a little more.

He looked at her again. "What happened at the last foster home?"

"Tame Campbell, I'll never forget that jerk. If I keep myself busy like I have been here lately then I don't think about it as much. He was a mean drunk, his wife wasn't much better, she always let me take all the beatings instead of getting them herself. I don't know how they fostered any kids ever. One night while I was in the room I slept in, he came in, with the most hateful look I'd ever seen, and he tried to climb on the bed with me…" She shuddered at the thought. "I didn't know what he had concocted in his mind but I knew it wasn't good, I grabbed the lamp next to the bed and slammed it into him, took a couple times but he finally fell off the bed. I ran, went to the only place I could run to, Candice's."

Eli's gaze snapped back to her, and she knew the disgusted look would be there so she looked away.

"They took me in for a couple of months while I looked for a job to support myself, no one came looking for me either, probably because they knew how much of a problem I was, me and my mouth were always in trouble. Candice never liked him, because of the stories I'd told her, so when that happened she didn't even ask her parents she just kind of moved me into her room and shared everything with me, her clothes, a space on her bed."

"Look at me," Eli demanded. She slowly turned to him waiting for the disgusted look, but it wasn't there. "You did the right thing you know, slamming that lamp into him, maybe he's the one doing this?"

"I don't know, I don't know how they would find me, unless they heard the news from Daryl, or anyone else Daryl told I suppose. They're at the bottom of the list because of them being the last home I stayed in, but I guess it is possible they want to get back at me for slamming a lamp into him, but I just don't know, Eli. I'm scared, and lost, I've never felt this way before, I've always had a plan for the most part.

"I got the job to support myself and as soon as I was able to, I moved out of Candice's house and surprisingly, with the Howells' help I found my own place, finished high school, during all that chaos I was never afraid, but I am now."

Eli looked to the girls who were done with their baby food, he grabbed the jars and set them back on the table along with the spoons and he pulled her into a comforting hug. She had never wanted anyone but Candice and she supposed Caleb to know about her troubled past, but now she was spilling her guts to Eli. And he wasn't running away.

"I am so sorry I didn't give you the time of day before, Andie, I really am, I was too stupid to see what was in front of me, but I am glad you've made yourself into a strong independent woman."

She wrapped her arms around his neck just savoring the feel of the comfort he was offering. She sighed and moved from his lap and began to clean the girls and their trays just as a knock fell to the front door. She held her breath as Eli walked down the hallway to answer it.

He greeted the person in a friendly tone, so must not be a threat.

She heard two sets of feet coming down the hall. Of course one was heavy with them being Eli's boots, the other set was soft that she had to strain to hear. She turned as the two walked into the kitchen. Eli made a beeline for her and the girls, he picked Lucy up and turned Andie toward the guest who showed up. Andie picked Lily up before Eli introduced the supper skinny, tall, blonde woman.

"Belle, Andie Malone, Andie, this is Belle Mayson, she's Dale Hank's girl, she's going to watch the girls while we get you three some more things."

Andie recognized her right away. "You work at the police station, you were at the front desk the night I went down there."

"Yes, I do. I am so sorry I didn't help that night, I'm really ashamed of myself, it was such a shock about Candice and Caleb. How are you doing?"

"I guess, as well as can be expected. Have you heard if they've gotten anywhere with who possibly killed them?"

"No, last I knew they were going to investigate you, but now that you're in trouble I guess they took you off the table."

Andie shot a look up at Eli, this was the woman he was going to leave the girls with?

"Belle, stop it, you know she didn't do it, no one could fake how messed up she was after looking at their bodies, it wasn't her, and if Murphy doesn't find out who it was I sure as hell will, now you're sure you're up for watching both girls?" Eli admonished.

"Yeah, shouldn't be a problem, everything will be fine."

"Okay, good, we'll be heading out in a few, I will set the alarm before we leave, if it goes off get a hold of Dale right away. We had an issue earlier but no sign of anything, if anything happens have Dale call me." Eli wrapped his arm around Andie and they headed down to the living room and placed the girls in the playpen. "You two behave for Belle," he kissed Lucy then took Lily and kissed her.

Andie kissed both girls also. "I'll be back soon, little ones, everything's going to be okay." But as soon as those words were out of her mouth a knot formed in her stomach. Was everything going to be okay? She sure wasn't going to be after all of this was over and she'd have to start fixing up the bakery and get on with her life away from Eli. He was in lust with her and it sucked because she almost had a flint of hope that maybe, just maybe he was falling in love with her. But there was no way, even if he would say he was, she wouldn't let him sacrifice himself from having a family. A real family. Not two babies already made, yes one of them were blood to him, but the other just wasn't going to be enough for him.

And not to mention Maisy would be disappointed in not having more grandkids, according to Candice, Maisy had wanted a whole flock and Andie didn't blame her one bit. She glanced up to Eli and he wrapped his arm around her as they made their way out to the hallway and out the door. He set the alarm like he said he would and led her over to his truck and helped her.

Her eyes widened when he cupped her chin and made her look at him, "Don't worry about space here, there's plenty of room, so anything you think Lucy or Lily might need we'll grab it okay?"

"Okay, the biggest thing I can think of right now is the highchair."

"All right, let's go, babe." He leaned down and pressed those seductive lips against hers making her toes curl instantly. Boy, yeah she was done for. No one had ever made her feel this way before and it scared her senseless. But she could revel in the feelings for a little while longer couldn't she?

Chapter 16

After that toe-curling kiss Eli put Andie up into his truck and they headed to her place. She glanced out the back of the truck, seeing the hand he had stationed outside the front door, Levi Helms. He was big and burly but she still worried about the girls.

But the hard glint in the man's deep green eyes should have been a little reassuring, that he wouldn't let anything happen to the girls, that he would protect them with his life, but it wasn't. "Are the girls going to be okay?"

Eli looked over to her then pulled her up against him, pressing his lips against her forehead, "They'll be okay, at the first sign of trouble Levi and Dale will call, same with Belle, and we'll be back here in three minutes flat."

She let out a sigh as she laid her head against his shoulder. She had to trust Eli, he loved the girls so much, this had to be okay.

She looked at the bakery as they drove by. "The cops are still there?" she questioned when she saw the cruiser.

"I guess so," he huffed a little as he pulled up into the driveway beside her car.

"What's wrong?" she asked as she looked at him.

"I want to know what's going on, but I'll stay with you."

She looked over to the bakery then back to the house. "I can go in and start to get things, you can go talk to them, I'll be okay."

He searched her eyes slowly and she hoped she didn't show any fear. "Are you sure?"

She glanced back to the house. "Yeah, I'm sure. If I don't feel safe I'll come get you, I doubt anything is going to happen, I'll be okay." She smiled at him then went to move to the other side of the truck. She was pulled back to face him and his lips crashed down onto hers.

He pulled back and brushed his hand against her cheek. "All right, I'll be back in maybe twenty minutes, darlin'."

"Take your time, Eli." She pushed away the giddy feeling that threatened to fill her heart and got out of the truck.

She hurried into the house and went through the living room first, she didn't grab much. She headed to the kitchen and grabbed all the baby food and formula she had, then some more bottles. She got it moved to the front door along with the high chair. She was shoving everything into cloth bags she used for shopping. She placed everything in the high chair then headed to the nursery. She went through the clothes she had for the girls and shoved them into three more bags then put them with the high chair, bottles, and baby food, and the few toys she figured would make the girls happy. She rushed to her room to get her own things.

As soon as she walked into her room she was slammed down to the ground on her back. Before she could scream a hand was smashed down over her mouth. She began to struggle until the metal barrel was shoved beneath her chin. She froze as it was pressed harder against her.

"That's right, don't move, there's a bullet in here with your name on it if you don't cooperate. Have you been talking to the uncle about money?" the raspy voice demanded.

She shook her head, landing her a blow to the side of her head from the gun and it was shoved beneath her chin again biting into her skin. It hurt along with the spot he had hit her with it but she refused to cry. The pain radiating through her skull was intense, she was almost seeing stars but she wouldn't show weakness.

"Are you going to?" he hissed out.

She shook her head again. She wouldn't give in to this jerk, nor would she let Eli. She racked her brain to place his snaky voice. But she was hit again causing another bout of dizziness.

Everything spun around her. But she managed to reach up and slug the man on top of her.

It made him slam his fist into her cheek but before she could let out any sound he slammed his hand back over her mouth. She began to struggle again.

"If you don't want a bullet in you, I suggest you do what I'm telling you to. Because if you're gone, what do you think will happen to your little girl? I'll tell you what will happen, she'll end up in the system just like you did. No one wanted you, and no one will ever want her, she'll bounce around just like you did, so you best choose your actions carefully."

That sent anger through Andie, how did he know so much about her? She bit the man's glove covered hand, hard, making him pull back and he let out a growl.

He slammed his fist into her again, she gripped his other wrist and pushed it away from her just as he squeezed the trigger sending a bullet through her bedroom window.

She screamed in fear, and the pain in her ear from the loud shot, and the sound of shattering glass. All she could hear now was ringing through her ears but she wasn't held down anymore. She got up as the man took off from the room. She debated with herself before she went after him.

She staggered trying to push the ringing and dizziness away and managed to grab on to his black hoodie. He spun and slammed the gun into her mouth. She stumbled backward but didn't let go, pulling the man down to his knees.

"Let go of me, bitch, if you know what's good for you," he yelled as he tried to shake her off of him.

Carl and Dean dove to the ground at the sound of the shot, but Eli knew the glass shattering sound and gun shot came from Andie's house.

He hauled Carl and Dean up, shoving them out of the bakery and all three of them rushed to the little gray house. He burst through the front door as his heart dropped along with his stomach when he saw Andie struggling with the man in the hallway.

He heard Carl yell something but all he could focus on was Andie and the man with the gun pointed at her head.

That didn't stop Andie from slamming her fist up into the man's nose.

Carl yelled something again and the man stood up quickly taking Andie with him. He pulled her body in front of him as a shield for himself.

Eli's stomach knotted as the masked man shoved the gun against Andie's temple, Eli moved closer but froze when he dug the gun harder into Andie.

"One wrong move, lover boy, and she gets it. It would be okay with me, she ruined everything for me, so even just killing her will be satisfying," the man hissed the threat as he backed toward the kitchen. "If you want me to start leaving your girl alone, I want two million. Then I'll be out of everyone's hair and won't harm her or the two babies."

Eli was flabbergasted, he wasn't worth even half of the two million this asshole was demanding. "But, I don't…"

He felt Carl tug on his arm, which made him look back at him and take in the shake of his head, Eli shut his mouth. He turned back to Andie and his eyes locked with her wide, fear-stricken eyes.

The man continued to back toward the kitchen. Apparently he got the lay out of the house before the attack but, then again, it wouldn't have taken much with the small house. This angered Eli so much along with seeing the blood trickle down from her head and the corner of her plump little mouth that just fifteen minutes before he had had under his own. He slowly followed them until the man was pressed back against the glass door out to the patio. The man told Andie to open it.

Eli watched as she moved her hand slowly back and managed to push the door open with one push.

The man glared at him. "Remember what I told you, the money or I hurt your precious treasures." The man pushed Andie toward him.

Eli caught her quickly but then he noticed the gun aimed at them. He dove sideways pulling Andie with him as three shots rang out through the tiny kitchen splintering the cabinets that were above them. He looked for Carl and Dean. They had dived out the doorway to the hallway. Eli heard the patio door slam shut and it was only him and Andie in the kitchen.

Eli heard Dean rattle something off as they rushed out the patio door. His main focus was Andie. He had managed to cover her body with his own but he wasn't crushing her. He leaned back onto his knees and helped her sit up.

He pulled her against his body, her legs between his spread knees since his thighs were on either side of hers. "Baby, are you okay?" he looked down at her. "Who the hell am I kidding, of course you're not." He shook his head as he closely looked her over. More bruises, a gash against the side of her head near her hairline, and a gash along the side of her mouth. "Come on, we're getting you home."

"I didn't get anything of mine," she whispered and winced at the movement of her mouth. He stood up, gently pulling her up with him. "Do you have everything for Lucy and Lil?"

She nodded her head gingerly.

"Okay, we'll figure out something else for you, I'm getting you out of here now." He scooped her up into his arms. As he headed to the front door he adjusted Andie, making her wrap her arms around his neck to free his other hand so he could grab the high chair. After making sure the coast was clear, he dragged it out behind him and. hurried to his truck. He put Andie in the truck, first and closed her door. He put the clothes, formula, baby food, and toys in the backseat then loaded the chair into the bed.

He almost ran to the driver's side and got in swinging the truck back out of the driveway, tires squealing against the black top. He knew he should probably take her to the hospital but he wanted to get her somewhere safer. He headed back to the ranch, calling the hands to make arrangements for keeping watch all night.

He had no clue who this ass hat was but he wasn't getting close to Andie or their babies. He glanced over to Andie at the thought of their babies. It didn't upset him, didn't scare him, it made him so happy at the thought.

And he'd do whatever it took to keep them safe.

Andie let out a muffled groan as her body rocked a little as he headed back to the ranch. She ached quite a bit and couldn't believe she fought off the man. She stared out the windshield, shocked, and her teeth began to chatter a little bit along with her body shivering.

"Hang on, baby, we're almost home," he said with reassurance as he placed his hand on her jean covered thigh.

She sighed a little but didn't respond. She kept running the raspy, snaky voice through her mind trying to place it but it just wasn't clicking. She let out a huff as she leaned her head back against the head rest.

"Hey, you okay?" Eli questioned, probing gently instead of full force.

"Yeah, I'm fine, really. I'm just at a loss, I don't know who's trying to do this."

"Well, hopefully, Carl and Dean can get him. If not, we will figure it out, together. I'm here and I'm not going anywhere, got it?"

"You don't have to be though," she whispered.

"I want to be, Andie, you're not alone anymore. After what just happened, I figured you'd understand you need someone on your side."

She turned her gaze on him, sending her head spinning. "And what happens to the girls if we're both hurt by this guy or taken out like he threatened?" She gritted her teeth. "Lily has grandparents, Candice was Godmother of Lucy, so I have no one to take care of her if something happens to me, except for you, and for that to happen I can't have you getting hurt or worse!" Tears slowly filled her eyes but she tamped them down before they spilled over.

They pulled up outside of the house and Eli put the gear shift into park and turned toward Andie. "And I don't want you or the girls hurt either, why on earth would you even think I'd be okay with you getting hurt?" Eli demanded sternly as he pulled her into him.

She sighed, would she ever be okay with the sternness that seemed to take over him instantly? She slowly pulled back from him when he went to cup her face in his hands, she pushed open the door of the truck and got out. Was she ever going to keep in line with Eli or was she always going to feel like she was getting herself in more trouble with him, even if it was just him showing he cared about her?

Her bottom was always going to be feeling the heat after having a talk with Eli if they pursued anything and she did indeed give in to how stern he could be and what the consequences would always be with him. She looked at herself in the glass window of the door and let out a sigh.

She headed inside and headed to the bathroom pushing the dizzying feeling away. She more than likely had a concussion but she needed to get cleaned up. She heard the giggles of the girls come from the living room. She turned a little almost ready to go to them but knew she had to get cleaned up first. She went into the bathroom and just stared at herself in the mirror. She had a circular bruise beneath her chin, a few more on her cheek, the ones on her neck were fading a tiny bit. Blood covered the side of her cheek from her head and down her chin to her neck from the side of her mouth. She placed her hands on the vanity top and looked down. Why couldn't she place that voice?

Eli watched Andie walk into the house. He got out of the truck, retrieved the high chair and the other items Andie had bagged up and carried them inside. He gave the girls their toys and kissed them as Belle stood from the couch. "What happened, Eli?"

"She was attacked at the house, Carl and Dean were in the bakery, I didn't get much out of them before we heard the shot from her bedroom, she fought him off though, they went after him."

Belle laid her hand on his chest. "Eli, she's going to get the girls and you killed."

He raised an eyebrow at her. "What? Do you know something?" he demanded.

"No, no, of course not, it's just obvious this person is really gunning for her and you keep getting in the way."

"Yeah, that's what you do for family," he answered shortly.

"But, what about the girls? Aren't they more important?"

"Everyone is important in this, including Andie, she's the mother of those girls."

"Oh, come on, we both know she doesn't have a claim to Lily at all."

"Well, obviously Candice and Caleb thought she did, and I have to accept that."

"But…"

"No, it's done." He frowned at Belle. "I'm taking care of all of them, no matter the cost."

Belle backed away from him a little. "Okay, fine, but I'm just saying, she's not been a good thing that's come to this town. I will watch the girls, because they are so precious, if you want but I do not respect her at all."

"I've never asked for respect from anyone in this stupid one-horse town," the soft voice came from the entrance into the living room. "I never asked for Candice to give me custody of Lily. I don't know why she gave it to me, or why Caleb agreed, but I will uphold their wishes, and if that means leaving, since no one wants me here, then that is exactly what I'll do. I don't care anymore. I've never had family before except for Candice, do you really think it would bother me to take care of those girls by myself? It's what I've been preaching to Eli since the day I was granted custody, or if he really wants Lily, then fine, he can have her and I will walk away." She glared at both of them then stormed into the living room, picked Lucy up and began to leave the room.

Eli stood there dumbfounded, what had he said wrong? He wanted to protect all of them not just Lily, he turned to Belle.

"I think it's best if you go for now, I'll let you know what's going on." He picked Lily up and headed after Andie and Lucy.

Andie rushed to the nursery and began to get some of Lucy's things but placed her in the crib so she could get everything she needed. She was so angry, he was doing this because of feeling like she was family. You didn't sleep with family and he had most definitely done that the night before. She began to shove things into the diaper bag.

She turned to grab more things but jerked back when she saw Eli standing there with Lily. She glared at him and went to pack more things. He placed Lily in the crib with Lucy. "What are you doing, Andie?"

"Leaving like everyone wants. I'll just start over some-where else, away from you and Lily, that'll keep you guys safe."

"And what about you and Lucy?"

"I'll keep us safe."

"Andie…"

"No, I'll go."

She let out a shriek when he turned her around and pulled her to him. "You're not leaving."

"You can't tell me what to do, and you're not going to." She tried to push him away from her. "You got what you wanted last night, I will just be on my way now."

"Oh, and what did I get?"

"Laid, and it will not happen again."

"Andie, stop it, that's not all I wanted."

"Then what all do you want, Eli?" she demanded as she glared up at him.

He pulled her up into his arms, held onto her and pressed

his lips to hers. "I want everything." He plundered her lips slowly and gently.

"Everything?" she mumbled as she looked up at him as he pulled back.

"Everything, Andie." He bent his head and kissed her again, making her toes curl. She felt him skim his hands down her back and cup her ass in his hands, wrapping her legs around his hips. "Do you think the girls will be okay for a little bit? The alarm is set and Levi is still posted outside, we need to get you cleaned up."

Andie glanced over to the girls as they played in the crib. "I guess they'll be okay," she whispered.

He headed out of the room, shutting the door a little. He went to the room they had slept in the night before and grabbed the monitor then carried her across the hall to the bathroom.

He sat her down on the white vanity top, crouched down and began to rummage under the sink. She watched him carefully as he pulled out a first aid kit

He stood up and spread her legs apart and stood between them.

Her breath hitched a little as he moved closer than necessary. He pulled out an alcohol swab and began to clean her open gashes.

She hissed in a sharp breath and grabbed his wrist. "That hurt," she mumbled.

"I know, baby, but it needs done, okay?"

She shook her head, refusing, he placed the pad on the counter and shook his own head. His hand came up to her cheek gently but she pulled away from him.

"Babe, I'm sorry I let my temper snap in the truck, and I'm sorry about Belle, and everything else. I never knew how many made you feel like an outcast and I was one of those once but I wasn't intentionally doing it, I made everyone feel that way, even my own brother while we were trying to get this place up and running." She let him touch her cheek this time. His fingers gently trailed the bruises and the gashes along her head and mouth. He tilted her head up a little and saw the bruise beneath her chin.

He moved closer and pressed his lips to it making her breath hitch all over again. This man was maddening. He kissed his way down to the bruises on her neck then back up to the ones on her cheeks. Then he brushed her lips with his. Her hands moved to his chest and moved up to around his neck digging her fingers in the back of his hair.

His hands landed on her hips and he pulled her against him as she let out a moan. He pulled back from her and their eyes locked. "Now, are you going to let me get you cleaned up?"

She nodded her head and he grabbed the alcohol pad and began to pat the gashes gently. She hissed but didn't pull back again. She looked up at him from under her lashes once he was finished. "What did you mean by 'everything'?" she whispered.

He nuzzled his nose against hers gently, then began to strip her shirt off of her. "It's just how it sounded, I want everything. You, Lily, Lucy, and to keep you guys safe and cared for, I don't want you to leave, I want you to stay here so we can be a family, a real family."

"You don't sleep with family," she whispered still not fully meeting his gaze.

He put a finger under her chin and tilted her head up. "You do if you're together, and I want that."

Her eyes widened at the shock, she felt her breath leave her lungs as she searched his eyes. The pounding of her heart entered her ears. Could he be serious? "You can't be serious," she whispered.

"And why not?"

"You don't want an already made family, you'll eventually want your own kids."

"I want you, Lily, and Lucy, if me and you want more kids then we can adopt, there are so many kids we could save to keep them from living the life you lived, or we can figure out a way for us to have one of own, we'll figure it out."

"Are you sure this isn't just because of the scare we had today?"

"I'm sure, not going to lie, my heart shattered when I knew there was nothing I could do, but why do you think that is?"

"Because then you'd be raising a little girl by yourself?" she offered.

"No, because I don't want to lose you, ever." His mouth clamped down on hers again and she reacted right away. She felt the warmth spread over her instantly as she clutched at his shoulders. She moved her hands to his buttoned-down, dark-blue shirt and began to pluck them open. She grazed her hands over his taut chest and further down across his six-pack and popped open the button on his light blue jeans.

She felt his mouth move from hers and attack her neck again and she arched up to him. His hands moved up her back rubbing gently sending goosebumps along her skin. She shivered and moaned as his hands moved around to the front of her and cupped her breasts gently, grazing her already hard peaks with his thumbs. She loved the feel of his rough skin against her soft one.

He pulled her down off the counter, undid her jeans and stripped her of them. He picked her back up, wrapping her legs around him and she felt his already bulging shaft press against her from behind his zipper. She reached between them and cupped him through his jeans making him hiss this time. "I need you to know I am being serious, Andie, I want everything. Including your obedience. I will be the head of our household. You'll have a voice but my word is final. Misbehavior will be followed by discipline but obedience will be followed by rewards. You'll want for nothing. You and our children will want for nothing. You will be treated as the treasure you are."

"I believe you," she mumbled and pressed her lips against his. She moaned from the pleasure of their lips nibbling each other's. "Eli, please," she whispered against his lips.

She rubbed against him making him groan. He pulled her harder against his arousal as he turned and pressed her up against the wall. "Are you sure?"

"Yes, I'm sure. I want this, I'm sure. I believe you. Please, Eli, I want you. I want it all," she gasped out as she dug her hands into his hair again.

He caught her hands and pressed them up against the wall too and shoved his pants down. She bit her lip as she leaned her head back against the wall, closing her eyes, he was making everything disappear. He seemed to be doing that a lot lately. Taking everything away that was bad. She felt his member brush against her burning center and then he entered her waiting opening.

She arched her back as he plunged into her, making her scream in pleasure. He leaned down and caught her quivering rose-tipped nipples, swirling his tongue around each in turn. His other hand sneaked between them and he began to twirl two fingers around her sensitive button making her climb even higher up the mountain of pleasure. She felt everything start to come undone around her quickly as her breath became more ragged when he moved back to her neck.

She screamed even more at the feel of the blinding, pulsing, moment of release coming so close. She tried to pull her hands from the one holding hers above her head as she jerked into his fingers increasing the pressure. She felt the clench deep inside her and convulsed into a chain of spasms, crying out his name.

Which followed his own cry of her name as he was brought

with her into his own spasms, spilling into her as he let out a harsh breath of satisfaction. He leaned his forehead against hers as they quivered against each other, their breath quick and shallow. He slowly pulled back from her but didn't put her down or pull her off of him. His eyes were so dark with desire, as if the last two times hadn't been enough. And she knew exactly how he felt.

He pressed a kiss to her forehead, still holding her hands. "So, are we doing this together?" he whispered.

She stared at him for a minute, could she let him in the way she had dreamed ever since Candice had started this ridiculous quest to get her and him together. She would have to let go of so much but she was thinking it would be a good thing for them. She slowly nodded her head and he kissed her again. She kissed him back, but she knew if it came down to him or her, she would sacrifice herself over him. And it may just come down to that if the cops didn't figure out who was doing this to her.

Eli slowly set her down on the floor, he started the shower and they got in to clean up. As soon as they got out Eli ran downstairs to get her one of his shirts and a pair of gym shorts, which she put on as soon as he came back to her.

They got the girls and began to fix supper, which was just macaroni and cheese but was still delicious, they got the girls fed, bathed, and ready for bed. With no questioning whatsoever from Eli they went to the same room as the night before and he held her.

She had to figure this out. The voice just kept replaying in her mind like a nagging old biddy but it just wasn't clicking.

Chapter 17

It had been a week since the attack at Andie's house. Everything seemed calm around them, but Eli still refused to leave the girls and her alone.

He kept her inside the house, she wasn't even allowed to start the clean-up at the bakery. He had made arrangements for a cleaning and a construction crew to start most of the repairs and cleaning. But since she was on lockdown she had to wait to redecorate the shop.

She stood in front of the huge windows in the living room, her arms wrapped around herself. How did everything in her life turn upside down? The cops had to let Daryl go, they found that the bullets from the bakery, and her house matched the ones that killed Candice and Caleb. She let out a sigh, the jackass was sloppy, just not sloppy enough.

"Andie," Eli's deep voice called from behind her, she turned away from the window a little. He sat a cranky Lily and Lucy down near their toys and made his way over to her and pulled her away from the window. "You know I don't want you in front of the windows."

"I know, I know, a bullet can shatter these windows and hit

me," she grumbled as she let him pull her away from the window and draw the curtain shut.

"Wow, all three of you are awfully grumpy today," Eli teased as he made Andie sit on the couch.

The girls began to crawl over to them and Andie pulled each one up on the couch between herself and Eli. "Well, I'm grumpy because everything is out of control, I can't even be outside or do anything I enjoy doing, I can't bake anything, you have nothing here for me to bake or I would be doing that, it relieves so much stress for me." She pressed a finger into Lucy's mouth then another into Lily's. "These two are cranky because they are cutting at least a tooth each." She kissed Lucy on the forehead then Lily and made her way down to the kitchen.

"You're coming back, right?" Eli called out quickly.

Andie rolled her eyes and chuckled a little, he did a lot for the girls, and loved them so much, but when it came to them being cranky, he seemed to panic a little. She went to the freezer and found what she was looking for, vanilla ice cream. She got two bowls with three spoons and began to dish it out.

She put the carton away then headed back to the living room. She smiled when she saw Eli trying to entertain the girls. "We should get them teething rings, I forgot to grab them. I didn't even think about it, I forgot a lot of things," she mumbled the last part.

She had been stuck in his t-shirts and gym shorts ever since the attack. She hated this, she wanted her own clothes, her own house. She sat down beside the girls and handed Eli a baby spoon.

"What? Where's mine?" he demanded with a little bit of a scowl but almost a pout.

"One bowl for them, one for us," she answered as she shifted to press her back against the arm of the couch and crossed her legs Indian style.

"I don't share too well you know," he warned.

Her eyes widened. "Are we still talking about ice cream?"

"Hmm, maybe." He smiled at her.

She rolled her eyes at him and began to feed Lucy some ice cream making her shriek a little and clap her hands. Andie smiled as Eli fed Lily some then he pulled the metal spoon out of her hand and took some out of their bowl.

The girls finished the bit of ice cream in their bowl and then she and Eli began to share theirs after they placed the girls on the floor to play. Andie let out a little squeal when a drip of ice cream fell onto her inner thigh.

Eli smiled at her and leaned forward slowly, licking it off, making her shiver and moan. He leaned away with a wicked grin still pasted to his lips, took another bite then gave her another spoonful.

He moved the spoon to her mouth slowly until some dripped onto her collar bone.

"Hey, you did that on purpose," she accused, frowning at him.

He smiled and leaned forward licking it off of her, making her moan again. "No, never," he whispered but instead of pulling away he pulled her against him as he pressed his lips against hers and placed the empty bowls on the side table behind her.

She whimpered, running her fingers through his hair as he continued to kiss her. He slid his hand beneath her shirt, resting it against her side.

Slowly they pulled away from each other, glancing at the girls making sure they were okay. He nuzzled his nose against her neck. "Apparently we should introduce ice cream into our bedroom." He teased her and pressed his lips against her neck again. "Tastes pretty good off of you, too."

She smacked his chest playfully and wiggled out from under him. "You're terrible, I swear you've locked me in your fortress for your own personal gain."

He went after her and pulled her back against him, his arm around her waist. "And what gain would that be?" he whispered against her ear.

"I haven't figured that out yet," she whispered back. She turned in his arms. "Can we go to the store? I need to get the girls some things, diapers, formula, baby food, and something for their gums to help with the teething, not to mention I need a few things."

He searched her eyes., "Okay." He gave in.

"Really?" she asked, shocked that he actually agreed.

"Yeah, I need some things too, so we'll take Levi with us and then we'll go." He turned to get the girls and headed back to the nursery where he changed them and came back to her.

Andie took Lucy but froze. "Oh no, we don't have any car seats for the girls, they're at my house in my car."

"Your car is out by my truck, I had Dale bring it here. You stay in here with the girls while I get the seats moved." He pressed his lips to her forehead, handed her Lily then headed outside.

That man never ceased to amaze her. She went back to the living room, sat down on the couch and began to make a list of everything she needed. It was a going to be quite a long list. She stared at the dark wooden and glass entertainment center and the forty-inch TV.

She wondered if she could talk Eli into letting her cook a decent meal. Spaghetti pie sounded so delicious with garlic knots and extra cheese. Good thing she knew the recipe by heart since she had eaten it almost every day during her pregnancy with Lucy.

A frown puckered her brow at the thought. But it was impossible. She shoved it away as Eli came back into the living room. He noticed right away. "What's wrong?"

She shook her head a little, "Nothing, just thinking about everything I want to get, I want to make a good meal tonight."

"Okay, babe." He walked closer to get Lily while she got Lucy. He placed his hand on her back possessively and protectively.

She didn't mind it either, she moved closer to him. He smiled down at her and she smiled back, his lips touched her temple. They headed out to the truck, he seemed to tense a little bit and so did Levi as he followed behind them.

"We don't have to do this if no one wants to," she offered.

Eli's gaze flicked to hers. "It's okay, just a little nervous and on edge but we'll be okay." He opened the passenger side and helped Andie up so she could put Lucy in her seat. He headed around to the other side to put Lily in her seat.

They got in the front seat, Levi jumped into the back with the girls. They headed to the store.

After they arrived and Eli had parked, Andie looked at him and said, "So, I was thinking we could split up, I'll take Lucy you can take Lily, that way we can both get what we need and it won't take as long."

Eli turned to look at her quickly, she had a feeling he wasn't going to go for it. She bit her bottom lip as she waited for his answer.

He reached out and tugged her lip from between her teeth, he leaned forward pressing his lips to hers. "Okay, but Levi goes with you."

"Okay, thank you, Eli."

He kissed her again and whispered in her ear, "If you don't stay with Levi and in his sight, there will be consequences. Do you understand?" She nodded eagerly. He turned to Levi, "You don't let her out of your sight."

"Yes, boss."

They got out and put the girls into shopping carts. Eli stuck close on the way inside then separated and Levi stuck to her like glue until she went down the feminine aisle. She got pads because she was due soon, and began to walk past the pregnancy tests, she shook her head, it wasn't possible. She couldn't be and even if she could it was impossible to even think about right now.

But something in the back of her brain was prickling at her but she just walked away. She found Levi standing at the end of the hair dye aisle.

She'd gotten all the ingredients for the spaghetti pie and the garlic knots, and everything the girls needed. She bit her lip a little, she loved being in Eli's shirt all the time but she was ready for her own things. She looked up at Levi when she stopped beside him, "I want to get some clothes too, is that okay?"

Levi looked around for a minute, she'd never seen such a big bulk of a man with such a bushy beard look so nervous. "All right, I'll hang around but won't hover."

"Okay, I'm sorry, Levi, but thank you."

He grunted and they made their way to the clothes and just like Levi promised he didn't hover. She picked out a few tank tops, shorts, some t-shirts, a pack of panties and a couple of bras. While she was still looking she slowed down a little bit when she adventured into the lingerie aisle.

Her heart sped up a little bit, she'd never worn these kinds of things nor shopped for anything like it before. Her heart was really jumping. She wondered if Eli would want her to wear anything like this. She nibbled on her lip for a minute. Her eyes kept scanning the lacy, barely there outfits.

Her eyes landed on a purple baby doll, it seemed the least inappropriate, but then again when you wore something like this, wasn't inappropriate what you looked for? The bodice was lacy material but wasn't see through but the rest was clearly flimsy and very see through. It would come down just to her thighs. And where it would cup her breasts there was a lighter, silk purple ribbon and bow. The band was thick, not skimpy like the straps.

She pulled it off the rack and hid it below the rest of the clothes along with a little longer black silk robe. This was a horrible idea. She just started to leave the aisle when she heard a loud voice shouting.

"I told you to keep an eye on her, Levi, this isn't keeping an eye on her! Now, where is she?"

"Eli, stop, I'm right here." She rushed out of the aisle and about ran right into Levi and Eli.

Eli turned and rushed up to her, cupping her cheeks and kissing her passionately, right there in the store with so many people to see. "What're you doing?"

"I just was picking out some things. Levi was giving me some privacy, but I'm all done now, so we can go if you're ready."

"Okay, did you get everything for the girls and yourself?"

"Yeah, everything I can think of for now anyways, I'm sorry for leaving Levi."

"We'll talk about it later, come on, let's get checked out so we can go home." He kissed her forehead and they went to the registers.

Andie began to go to a different line when Eli grabbed her arm. "Where are you going?"

"To check out, obviously."

"I thought we were doing that together." Eli frowned at her.

"I've got it, Eli, really."

"But…"

"No, it's okay, the girls are my responsibility."

"Well, that's where you're wrong, they are both our responsibilities."

She let out a sigh. "Yeah, and the bakery was mine and you've already taken care of those bills, so let me handle this stuff."

He closed his eyes and she was waiting on the argument, "Okay," he mumbled. "But keep Levi close to you."

She nodded her head and headed to the other open self-checkout. She began to ring everything up.

Eli still kept an eye on all three of his girls. They definitely had a few things to work out between them. They were a team when it came to a few things, other things not so much.

He finished his check-out and waited for Andie to finish up.

As soon as she was done and walked over to them, they headed out to the truck and got everything loaded up. He couldn't help but feel Andie was acting a little nervous or strange.

But he decided to keep his mouth shut in front of Levi. They got the girls loaded up then they headed home. Andie went to get the girls settled in the playpen, she grabbed her bag that she had put her clothes in and put them in the bedroom she'd been staying in. Then she came out to the kitchen, she laid her hand against his chest and said, "Why don't you go relax while I put supper together?"

He searched her eyes and pulled her closer to him, he brushed the back of his fingertips against her cheek. "Are you sure?"

"Very sure, you go play with the girls and I'll handle supper." She smiled up at him and she looked happy.

He ran his fingers through her hair. "Okay, baby, if you need anything let me know." He leaned down and kissed her passionately again. He seemed unable to keep his lips, hands, and everything else off of her. He headed out to the living room and climbed into the huge playpen which took up one whole corner of the living room.

Andie's heart felt like it was about to burst out of her chest. What had she been thinking when she picked up that silly little thing at the store? And little was being generous. She began to throw everything together quickly and threw it into the stove to bake. She headed out to the living room to wait for the stove to go off. As she walked in, her eyes landed on Eli and the girls playing. And she was stunned when she heard her baby's first word, "Da-da." And Lucy was looking right at Eli.

Andie could admit to herself that it was a shock, but it made her heart speed up even more. She smiled at the interaction Eli was giving both of the girls but he was especially thrilled when Lucy said da-da. He looked up and saw Andie, he jumped from the floor and stumbled out of the playpen.

"Andie, I'm so sorry,"

"Eli, it's fine." She walked up to him and wrapped her arms around him tightly.

He tilted her head up with a finger under her chin, "You're sure?"

"Yes, there's no one else I'd rather have her call dad, I mean unless you don't want it. I'm sorry, I should have thought about that, if you don't want it I understand." She backed away from him quickly. She was such an idiot. So what he was thrilled that Lucy called him dad, it didn't mean he really wanted it. She spun around to head back to the kitchen.

She felt his hand grab her arm and spin her back around, she looked up into those wonderful golden eyes of his. "It's okay, Andie, I want her to call me dad, it's fine."

"But that's probably not a good idea is it?"

"Why isn't it a good idea?"

"I don't know, Eli. I really don't, what happens if something happens between us?" she tried to fight the tears at the thought. She hated thinking something could happen to them.

"Well, I mean something is happening between us, and I feel like it's working so far. I know it's happened faster than it normally would have due to everything that's going on, but it was bound to happen."

"Wait, that's why we're happening?"

"What's why?"

"Because of everything, because I got Lily, Candice and Caleb are gone, and then the jerk who's trying to find me and get you to pay him off?"

"No, that's not why. I eventually would have opened my eyes, may have been when I really got this place up and running off the ground but Caleb was always very persistent about you, but you know how stubborn I am."

She looked away from him a little and stared at the light wooden paneled wall behind him. She was so confused all of a sudden. What was happening right now? She frowned as she went to leave again. But he caught her and pulled her to him. She flattened her hands against his broad, muscular chest and looked up at him.

"Andie, I'm sorry it took me so long to get my head out of my ass, but if I would have listened to Caleb and taken the opportunity two years ago, I would be right here with you, right now, just like this, loving you and Lucy," he rambled out.

He just said loving, did he really mean he loved her? She looked up at him and searched his eyes, and said, "Eli?"

"Yes, I said loving. I love you, Andie, and I love Lucy," he looked into her eyes. "I want to be her dad and I want to be Lily's dad, and I want to be the one person you can always count on for the rest of our lives."

She was speechless, she had never had a man tell her he loved her. She searched his eyes a little bit more but didn't know what to say. Did she love him? So much that she could tell him she loved him too? The next thing she knew the oven timer began to go off and the girls began to get a little fussy. She turned away quickly to go get the girls.

"Andie, Andie, stop, it's okay, I'll get the munchkins, you go get the oven." He kissed her and she kissed him right back.

But did that mean she was ready to admit she loved him? Her head was spinning. She had to figure this out and quickly. She didn't want to know what life would be like again without him. She feared they would end. She bit her lip as she pulled out the pie and sprinkled it with the mozzarella cheese then placed it back in and began to put the garlic knots in the oven as well.

She turned to start preparing the girls' food when Eli walked in with them both and Lucy was chanting da-da. She shook her head as he put them in the high chairs and he began to help her get things ready. The stove began to go off again, she turned to get it and ran smack dab into Eli stumbling backward but he caught her and pulled her up into him. "Hey, you okay?"

"Yeah, I'm fine," she replied and locked eyes with him as her arm wrapped around his neck. "I love you too," she whispered as their eyes gazed deeply into each other's.

He smiled and leaned down, catching her lips passionately, she returned the kiss with as much passion and hunger. He slowly pulled back a little.

"I have to get the oven," she whispered.

He let her go to get everything out of the oven, when her phone began to ring loudly in her back pants pocket. "Eli, can you get that for me?"

"Yeah, where's it at?"

"Right back pocket."

He slipped his hand into the pocket pulling out the phone but cupped her ass with his other hand. She jumped a little but turned to smile at him.

"Hello?"

She hated not being able to hear the other side of the conversation.

"Um, yeah, hold on, she's getting food out of the oven, just a minute, Rose."

Andie placed the things on the stove to cool and spun around raising her eyebrows at him, "Rose?" she asked.

He nodded his head and handed her the phone.

"Hello?"

"Andie, thank God, I got ahold of you, have you seen Tame Campbell? His wife was just here and said he's been missing for a week, and she's actually worried about you." Rose's voice sounded frantic.

Andie stumbled to sit in the closest kitchen chair. "I'm sorry, why would his wife be worried about me, and he's missing like how?" She glanced at Eli fear gripping her heart.

He sat down beside her, laying a hand on her knee gently, with a frown on his face.

"She thinks he may be coming after you, she's divorcing him. She was feeling he was becoming a worse alcoholic and couldn't get over what you had done to them."

"What I did? I didn't do anything to them, all I did was defend myself that night, and run away."

"They lost their ability to foster any more kids, and since he was only in it for the money they lost all their income. When she filed for divorce, he took off and no one's heard from him around here. I'm so worried about you, Andie, and Lily and Lucy."

Andie flicked her gaze to Eli then laid her head in her hand. "We're fine, um, he may already be here. I've been staying with Eli, and Lucy and Lily are here also, we're safe here. I'm going to call the police and tell them everything you just told me, thank you, Rose."

"You're welcome. We have more news that's not so serious,

we found a small house down there close to Maisy and Todd and we're really thinking about taking it."

"That's great, Rose, that'd be great for Lily." She mumbled as her head spun even more. How was she going to get through this?

After she ended the call with Rose Howell, she called the police station, she asked for Carl or Dean since they were at the bakery the day she was attacked. She explained everything to them and they assured her they'd look into it. She ended that call and stared at the floor.

"Sweetheart?" Eli probed.

"They think it might be the last foster family I stayed with, the man, not his wife, apparently she's divorcing him, I guess he blames me for them getting kicked out of the foster system, that explains everything, oh my God, that's how he knew I was in the system and threatened that the same thing would happen to Lucy, that's how he knew no one wanted me."

"Hey, hey, hey," he said and pulled her into his lap and kissed her. "He's wrong. I very much want you, Andie. I love you. He's not getting to you, Carl and Dean know now, so we'll figure this out, it'll be okay, and nothing is going to happen to Lucy, she's going to be safe along with Lily."

She laid her head on his shoulder, the tears slowly rolled down her cheeks as he held her and rubbed her back. "I don't know what I'd do without you, Eli, thank you, for everything."

"Shh, it's okay." He kissed her cheek.

She calmed down some and they got the girls fed, then ate themselves. Eli got the girls ready for bed while she cleaned up the kitchen. She smiled at the thought when she told Eli she loved him and he said he loved her. Butterflies erupted through her stomach. She felt a pair of arms wrap around her waist and lips press against her neck. "What're you doing?" he whispered in her ear.

"Nothing, just getting this cleaned up and getting ready to go take a shower."

"Oh, is that an invitation?" he huffed out as he brushed his lips against her ear right before he nibbled on it.

She moaned as heat stirred inside of her, she leaned her head back against him. "Not tonight, Eli, you take your shower while I take mine, it's up to you if you want to stay the night with me again."

"Baby, I just told you I love you not too long ago, you're not getting rid of me that easily, I will meet you in the bedroom, we should maybe decide where we officially want to stay."

"I can't stay in Candice and Caleb's room." She jerked away from him a little.

"Hey, calm down, it's okay, I know. I'm not asking you to, but I'm thinking about doing some renovations around here."

"Oh?"

"Yeah, but you look so tired, you go take your shower and we'll get to bed." He hugged her and kissed her gently then headed down to the basement.

She let out a shaky breath and rushed to her bedroom, she hoped she wasn't making a mistake by doing this. She grabbed the new outfit and robe she had bought and flew into the bathroom she had been using.

She undressed quickly and jumped into the shower. Her hands trembled so badly she almost couldn't shave but she managed it. She washed, got out, and dried. She looked at herself in the mirror as she dried her hair.

As her eyes raked over herself she began to wonder what Eli really saw in her. At least she wasn't as messed up like she was a week ago. The gashes were healing pretty well. She finished drying and began to brush her hair, she put it up into a loose ponytail but left a couple tendrils hang along the sides of her face.

She turned to grab the new outfit – if that's what you

wanted to call it — when there was a light knock on the door. "Yeah?" she answered, her voice trembling as much as her body was.

"Hey, you okay in there?" Eli's husky voice flowed through the light wooden door.

"Um, yeah, fine."

"Are you sure?" he asked again.

The butterflies floated around in her stomach. "I'll be out in a minute, I promise."

"All right, baby."

She let out a shuddering breath as she heard him walk away. She finished getting dressed, pulled on the robe, and tied the sash around her body. She walked to the door, took a deep breath and leaned her head against it. Was she ready for this? What if he didn't like it? What if he only said he loved her because of everything she was feeling? She wrapped her fingers around the doorknob, turned it and headed to her room. She bit her lip as she hung around in the hallway for a minute.

She took another deep breath. *"You can do this,"* she whispered to herself. She slowly walked to the doorway and stood there. She began to feel a little nauseous, what if he hated it? What if everything was a huge mistake? So many things were uncertain, including this brave act. She was driving herself mad and didn't know what to do about it. She just lurked outside the door. Was this the right thing to do? She wouldn't know until she tried. But, at the same time, she was too scared to try.

Chapter 18

Eli lay on the bed, staring at the ceiling, one hand behind the back of his head. He was getting even more worried about Andie. She sounded so scared when he talked to her through the bathroom door.

Then again, she had every right to be. But he had no idea how to make her safer than what he was already doing. He rubbed his hand over his face, then pinched the bridge of his nose as he let out a sigh. But then a smile formed, Lucy had called him da-da, and it hadn't made him freak out. It had made his heart soar, and having Andie tell him she loved him was an amazing feeling too. Everything seemed to be falling into place.

He knew how frustrated she was by being cooped up and understood, but he didn't see any way around it. He wouldn't let the woman he loved fall into the hands of the evil asshole that wanted her, at least wanted to use her to get money.

He heard a sound at the door, his head jerked up and his eyes widened at the beautiful sight before him. She'd put her hair up a little and the silky looking, black robe was enough to get his blood roaring. He swallowed hard imagining what was beneath it.

His gaze raked over her, particularly her bare, tan legs which he knew were so soft and smooth. He couldn't wait to get his hands on her and rub his way along every smooth part of her body. His eyes widened a little more when her small, delicate hands reached for the sash around her waist and untied it. It fell open and he almost couldn't stay on the bed. She slowly let the robe drop to a small heap behind her.

His mouth dried as he gazed at her almost naked body, ready to pounce. He wanted to snatch up his little purple minx and throw her on the bed.

She began to bite that plump bottom lip of hers and he wanted to take over the job. "You hate it, don't you?" she mumbled and looked down at the carpet twiddling her fingers.

"Andie, come here," he rasped out. How could she possibly think he hated it? God, she was so beautiful. His gaze didn't leave her as she walked closer, he sat up leaning back against the sleigh frame.

His smile got bigger when she stopped at the side of the bed and stared at the comforter. He was surprised he wasn't making a tent with his aching bulge that he definitely couldn't ignore. "On the bed."

She climbed up onto the bed but stayed on her knees, staring at her hands as she laid them in her lap.

"Look at me, Andie," he coaxed quietly.

She shook her head a little.

He snuck his arm around her waist, tugged her forward and helped her straddle him. With his index finger under her chin, he tilted her head up. "Why would I hate this?" he asked as he ground against the core of her above him.

Her eyes widened as she wriggled against him.

"Why did you do this?" he whispered as one of his fingers

trailed along her silky skin following the strap and the cups of the baby doll.

"I-I don't know. I never... I just thought–" She stumbled over her words.

"Well, I'm definitely not hating it," he told her gently as he led her hand to his strained erection. "It's so hard not to burst right now. There's no one else like you, Andie, I want to drive home so bad right now." He pulled her closer and caught her lips just before he rolled her to her back. His blood boiled in a good way as all he could think about was devouring her. "I love whatever you wear, baby, or the lack thereof." He pressed his lips to her neck making his way down slowly.

He felt her body tremble beneath his, she arched up as his hand slid beneath the flimsy outfit to her center and stroked her softly. His lips trailed along her collarbone then down her cleavage. He pulled the cups down with his teeth, which pushed her round globes together more and he took both rose-tipped pebbles into his mouth, sucking hard as he drove his fingers into her tight wetness.

She screamed as she bucked onto his fingers. It had taken all his restraint not to take her against the bedroom wall the minute she had walked into the room, and he knew he wasn't going to last long once he buried himself deeply inside of her.

"Eli, please," she begged as she ran her fingers through his damp hair. He moaned when she tugged a little.

He felt her try to pull him to her lips, but instead he caught her hands, pinning them above her head, making her moan louder. He pressed his lips to her neck moving down slowly. He let go of her hands and moved to torture each one of her full globes and their rosy peaks.

He felt her scoot down and he pulled back a little. "Don't make me tie you down," he huffed out.

She looked at him wide-eyed., "You wouldn't," she gasped, her voice husky with sexual need.

"I will if you don't stop moving, I'm taking my time with you tonight. My sweet, wicked time." He started over making her squirm beneath him, trying to get him to slide into her. He was so close but instead he got off the bed and headed over to the silk robe and pulled off the sash. He wished he had enough to restrain her legs too, but it would just be enough for her wrists, hopefully it would keep her still enough.

He walked over to her and tied her wrists together gently then moved her body sideways a little and tied the other end around the frame. "There now you can't move too much." He locked eyes with her and he didn't see fear, he didn't think it was possible to see her eyes get darker with desire but they did. He bent over kissing her upside down. "Should I go get the ice cream too?" he teased.

She shook her head.

"Are you going to be good now?" He smiled when she nodded her head. He walked around the bed his shaft aching to get inside of her. He began his torment all over again, making his way down her beautiful, sexy body.

His fingers found her slick opening and began to thrust into her while he kissed down her body again.

She bucked beneath him almost causing him to forget about taking his time. He finally came to his destination, he slammed his fingers into her deeply as his tongue assaulted her sensitive sweet spot repeatedly.

Andi jerked as her body began to quiver at the manipulation from Eli's fingers and tongue. Strange she wasn't scared when he restrained her wrists with the sash from her robe, it only heightened her sensitivity. Although, she shouldn't be so surprised because most of their love making had consisted of him pinning her wrists down with his hands and it never bothered her, it turned her on even more.

She felt herself buck beneath his tongue and was so close to crossing the bridge of pure ecstasy. Breathing hurt her lungs but the air was forced from her at the same time. She wanted more, so much more. "Eli, please!" she cried out, wiggling in a frenzy. She needed him inside of her, deep inside her. Every one of her nerves were on edge, "Elijah!" she screamed.

She sucked in a startled breath as his mouth and fingers left her and were replaced by his long, thick shaft. She gripped the sash in her hands as her body racked with spasm after spasm.

He untied her wrists quickly and crushed her to his body, letting her hold onto him by wrapping her arms around his neck as he slammed into her, finally sending her over, crying out his name as he stiffened above her and released himself into her.

He leaned his forehead against hers as they shivered, coming down from the wave of passion between them. As their breaths and heartbeats settled down he stripped her completely bare and pulled her against the hard planes of his chest, his fingers rubbing tiny circles against her back.

"That was fantastic, Andie. Thank you for thinking of me when you bought the sexy nightie. You look beautiful in it," Eli said.

"I'm glad you like it, I still can't believe I got up the nerve to buy it," she giggled.

"I'm happy you did but that is something we need to discuss," Eli responded.

Andie felt the mood change a bit.

"What did I tell you when I let you shop on your own, today?

And now she knew why. "I was supposed to stay with Levi."

"And…" he prompted.

"And in his sight. I'm sorry, Eli! It'll never happen again, I promise!

"I appreciate the promise, baby. But do you know how I felt when I found Levi but you were not with him? The fear I experienced when I thought someone may have grabbed you?"

"I was only right around the corner!"

"Were you in his sight? Could he see around the corner?"

She really didn't want to answer this question. She knew she was sealing her fate, but she couldn't lie. "No, sir. I'm sorry, Eli." Her tears began to flow.

"I can't let this go, baby. I wouldn't be the man you need or the security you desire if I ignored this. Do you understand, Andie?"

"Yes, sir."

"Let's get this done," Eli began as he started to sit up. Andie began to sit up as well and Eli said, "Don't go anywhere, you're going to lie right here across my lap."

Andie gasped as Eli positioned her. "I'm what?"

"I know this is new for you, Andie. Do you trust me? Do you know how much you mean to me? How much I love you? What it would do to me if something happened to you? This is loving correction given to you by my heart and my desire to keep you safe, rules are in place for a reason. I would never truly hurt you. You know that, right?" Eli explained, all the while rubbing his hand across her perfect bottom.

Now Andie was truly crying and feeling so much guilt for her actions. How could she have been so blind to his need to protect her and so callous in regard to the way he would feel if she had been hurt? "I know you love me and I didn't understand earlier, but I completely understand now and I feel like a horrible person for scaring you so. I love you, Eli and I'm ready. Will you hold me after?"

"Of course, I will, baby!" And with that, he began spanking and lecturing, "When I give you a rule or an instruction, it's for your benefit and safety. I won't ever tolerate you disregarding your safety. This will be the outcome every single time you do so. I don't enjoy making you cry but attending your funeral would be far worse." He spanked and spanked, hoping to make a lasting impression.

Andie thought her butt was going to catch fire, it hurt so bad. But her heart was hurting so much worse. "I'm sorry! I'm sorry! I promise I won't ever break your rules again! Eli, please no more." And with that last plea, Andie collapsed in full surrender to Eli's punishment.

Eli felt the moment she accepted her due, and he breathed a sigh of relief. He stopped spanking and rubbed gently, whispering words of love until Andie stopped crying. He pulled her up in his lap, taking care her bottom was off the edge of his lap. She sniffled and hugged him tight. He held her for a bit then scooted down so they were both lying down, her head on his chest and their arms wrapped around each other.

She snuggled closer, "I love you, Eli."

He wrapped her in his arms, "I love you, Andie." He kissed her forehead, and they began to fall asleep.

Chapter 19

"I don't understand why I have to stay cooped up still, Eli, it's been two weeks, they can't find Tame or Daryl, I'll still stay here with you, I just want to bake, please, and Rose and Bruce are coming here to live in the next couple of days, I want to help them settle in." Andie locked eyes with the man she'd lost herself to two years ago. His eyes were dark at the moment, but she didn't back down.

She shivered as he strolled over to her slowly those eyes a more russet tint, she knew he was upset and to tread carefully or she wouldn't sit comfortably for a bit. "I want you safe and being out isn't going to be safe."

"Eli, please, I need to do something," she pleaded. She squealed when he pulled her up against him. Her feet were off the ground. He walked her back to the couch.

He laid her down on it and laid down on top of her. "I could just tie you down and keep you entertained."

Her stomach clenched at the thought. "No, Eli, I want to help Rose and Bruce and get the bakery painted." She tightened her fingers on his tight white t-shirt trying to fight the ache that swarmed inside of her. "All this doing nothing is catching up to me, I'm gaining so much weight."

He cocked an eyebrow and his hand began to roam all over her body. "Really? I can't tell," he whispered. He began to kiss along her neck.

"Please, Eli?" she pouted and did big puppy dog eyes when he looked at her.

He leaned back onto his knees. "Fine."

"Really?"

"Yeah, but," he pointed his index finger at her, "the minute you get any bad feelings you call the cops and me. Promise me, because you know there will be consequences, if not."

She sat up and threw her body into him wrapping her arms around his neck tightly making them teeter off the couch to the floor, she pressed her lips to his passionately, "Thank you, thank you, thank you."

"Yeah, yeah, as long as you promise."

"Of course, you have my word," she cupped his scruffy face, he had neglected to shave the past couple of days, it sent tingles along her hands. "I promise, Eli, thank you for letting me do this. I also was thinking, I know Belle doesn't like me, and quite frankly I don't care, I had my best friend, I don't need someone to replace her, but she did say she'd watch the girls. If she still wants to I can pay her for her time spent here to watch them."

"I'll handle all of that, baby, you worry about getting the bakery up and running. I'll tell Dale to have her give me a call, have her come over and I can hash things out with her then we can go to the bakery for a bit to figure out what you'd like to do with it okay?"

She let out a little huff, he gave in to her request so she would give in to his, at least this time he was asking, "Okay."

They separated while he talked to Dale then Belle, Andie went to check on her little girls. She let out a yawn as she watched them. The last few days had been rough, it seemed no matter how much she slept or how good she slept, she was still so tired.

She still hadn't let him talk about his idea of the master bedroom upstairs. She just couldn't bring herself to talk about it yet. It still seemed so fresh even with the nightmares gone since she'd been in Eli's safe, warm embrace at night.

She let out a sigh as she leaned her head against the frame. For a fleeting moment she wondered what it would be like to have another baby, maybe a boy. But it didn't last long when she felt a body came up behind her. She moved back into the familiar warmth. "So what's the verdict?"

"She'll be here soon, are you okay?" He wrapped one arm around her shoulders and kissed the top of her head.

She turned around, laid her head against him and wrapped her arms around him. "I'm okay," she whispered and fought the tears. He didn't need to know what she'd just been thinking.

He tilted her chin up and looked at her deeply. "You know you can tell me, right?"

"Yeah, it's nothing though."

"Okay." He looked in on the girls then took her toward the living room. He sat down on the couch and pulled her down on his lap. He brushed a hand against her cheek. "I want to talk about the master bedroom."

"Eli, please, no."

"Babe, just hear me out, I don't want to change it, I don't know how long we'll keep it the same but we can for as long as we need to, but I want to make one little change, we can close it off from the bathroom, then open it up on from the other bedroom beside it, then we can move into that one." He rubbed her thighs as she nestled against his semi-hardness.

She pursed her lips. "I guess that would be okay, do I get to decorate our room?"

His eyebrows raised a little. "Sure, why not."

"Okay." She laid her head down on his shoulder as he wrapped his arms around her.

Andie took a deep breath as Eli pulled up in front of the bakery. The huge window was replaced and so was the logo and Andie's Sweets.

"Hey, you okay?" Eli touched her arm.

"Yeah, it looks good," she whispered. "Thank you for fixing it, Eli."

"I'd do anything for you, including catch you from a falling ladder."

"Well, I guess it's a good thing I brought you. If I paint today you'll be there to catch me if I fall."

Eli moved to the middle seat and put an arm around her shoulders then dipped his head, plundering her lips as he laid his other hand against her cheek. "I'll always catch you, even if you're not on a ladder."

She wrapped her arms around his neck. "I know, I'm slowly learning and the same goes for you."

"Thanks for the offer, baby, but I might squish you if you try to catch me from falling off of a ladder."

She tilted her head up and smacked his shoulder. "That's not funny."

He broke into a full smile. "I can't help it you're so tiny."

She frowned at him. "I am not, you're a jerk." She turned to open the door. She was snatched back and he pulled her sideways over his lap her back against the driver seat and he leaned down toward her.

Her breath hitched as his lips brushed hers and her hands cupped his cheeks as the kiss deepened. He slowly pulled back. "And this is why I like you being tiny, I can put a smile on that beautiful face of yours when I easily put you in these types of positions."

She rolled her eyes at him and tried to fight the smile he had just mentioned. "Come on, cowboy, let's get inside so I can decide what to do now that it's all fixed up."

He tilted her back up into his lap, opened the door, and scooted over, putting her arms around his neck, he carried her to the bakery. She giggled a little as they went inside.

He sat her up on the counter next to the register and the giggle died as her eyes fell all around them. There were so many patched up places along the walls, ruining the light gray walls with little pink iced vanilla cupcakes that Candice had painted. Tears filled her eyes and before she knew it the tears flowed down her cheeks. Her heart ached so badly.

Eli turned to see the tears, he tilted his hat up a little then moved between her legs, he wrapped his arms around her tightly. "I know, baby."

"It's all gone, Candice and I worked so hard on this place," she sobbed out. "She worked so hard on the cupcakes, it's all gone, and I can't get it back."

He rubbed the back of her neck beneath her hair with his fingertips. "I know, baby, I want to make it all better, I really do," he murmured and he tensed a little when she wrapped her arms around him, clutching his shirt tightly. He was such a fool when he thought she didn't care or wasn't upset.

Everything was still eating her up inside, and every day she put on a show. He laid his cheek against the top of her head letting the rose and vanilla scent encase him. He just let her cry it all out, even though it wouldn't fix anything but it might lessen the pain a little bit.

After a little bit she pulled back, her body not trembling as bad, but she didn't let go of his shirt. "I'm sorry I made your shirt all wet."

"No big deal, sugar, but guess what?" he whispered cupping her cheeks.

"What?" She sniffed a little.

He sighed, her cheeks were red and puffy and her beautiful eyes weren't much better, they were so wide with vulnerability. "You crumpled and I was right here to catch you."

She pressed her cheek against his hand. "I'm sorry, but thank you."

He brushed his lips to hers then nuzzled her pert little nose, gently. "Any time, babe, any time, maybe this was too much, too soon," he whispered.

Her eyes darted around quickly then looked back up at him as he rubbed his thumb against her cheek. "I'm just going to do a powder blue I guess, and be done with it," she whispered.

"Baby, we can wait a little longer if you want. I'll let you bake me all kinds of things at the house, I'll buy anything you need or want."

She glanced around again. "No, I just want to go home." She whispered.

"Babe…"

"No," she whispered and started to get off the counter, he helped her down and took her back out to the truck.

"Do you at least want to go pick out the paint?"

She looked over at him. "Eh."

"Andie, what's the matter? It's more than the bakery isn't it?"

"No, I'm fine."

"Andie, I've told you before not to lie to me," he said firmly.

She let out a sigh and tears began again. "It should have been me, I don't know why but I feel like it should have been me, at least they could have had more kids. I don't have anything to offer you, why would you love someone like me?"

"Andie, hey, hey, no, come here." He moved over to her and pulled her into him. "I love you because you make me laugh, you irritate the piss out of me but it's a good thing, you haven't acted like a robot around me, and you're not afraid to tell me off when there are so many people who are, you gave me Lucy ten months ago, we just didn't know it yet, we have Lily, we have two very beautiful daughters and we are a family, baby, you're a wonderful mother to those two little girls, and we just fit together perfectly."

She continued to cry as she leaned against him, there was something else going on with her and he had no clue what, he just held her all over again until the tears stopped. "Hey, I've got an idea, Belle's still watching the girls, she thought we were going to paint, why don't we go on a ride?"

"Like on horses?" she sobbed out a little.

"Yeah, why not?"

"Okay, why not?"

He smiled down at her. "Only if you want to, babe."

"It sounds fun, so yeah, let's do it."

"Okay."

They headed back home, once they arrived they headed to the barn and Eli got two horses tacked up, he helped her up onto the horse then got on Lightning. He took her hand gently as they rode along the well-worn trail. He couldn't keep from glancing at her. He didn't know what to do for Andie anymore, he bit his cheek as he thought. "We could always adopt," he suggested.

Her head whipped back to him. "I'm sorry, what?"

"I'd be happy to adopt if you want more kids, babe."

She turned away from him. "Honestly, I don't know what I want, actually I do, I want my best friend back. I want my life to go back to the way it was before."

"Like when I wasn't in it?" he snapped.

"No, Eli, that's not what I meant." She pulled back on his hand but he shook her off quickly. "Is it just the baby thing or are you realizing you really don't want to be with me?"

"Eli, that's not what I said."

"Could have fooled me, I'm going back."

"Eli, please." But he took off before she could finish.

He was so angry and knew he was going to lose his temper with her, he'd done good to keep it in check lately and he didn't want to lose it right now, she was emotional, was letting everything out. He froze and turned his horse back around and kicked him into a canter. He found her off of the horse and just standing there crying a little bit.

He jumped off the horse quickly, ran up to her and said, "Andie, come here, please?" Not making a move toward her.

She looked at him and she looked so hurt, but he didn't make a move toward her, he waited for her to come to him but instead she stepped back from him instead, "No."

"Andie, I'm sorry."

"I don't care, just know we're moving back out, it seems safe to me and I'll get the bakery opened back up and everything, all by myself."

"Andie, don't leave."

"You wouldn't want someone who really doesn't want to be with you, I've let myself free with you but I don't want to be with you."

"Andie, listen to me, I'm sorry, I didn't mean it. I know everything is getting to you and I am so sorry, I was being an asshole, please, I know you love me and I love you."

She glared at him but didn't move away when he walked closer to her, she let him wrap his arms around her. "Why would you think I don't love you?"

"Because I'm an idiot, because I can't say or do anything to make all of this go away, but I need you to do me a favor."

"What?"

"Think back to when you found out you were pregnant with Lucy."

"What about it?"

"Everything, just think of everything when you first found out."

"Yeah I don't feel the same way. Why would you even bring this up? You know I can't."

"Why, because a couple crackpot doctors told you that you couldn't? Those same doctors tell you that before? Because if they did then they are a bunch of crackpots because, for crying out loud, you had a kid, we could try, Andie, if that's what you really want we can try, I'll find you the best doctors so we can figure this out."

"But why hope? What's the point of hoping just to get shut down? I hoped once, I hoped you would like me when Candice told me how great you were, that was two years ago. It took two years for you to fall for me and it took me being guardian over Lily to make that happen. What if this us having a baby thing takes too long and takes its toll on us and we end up fighting even worse than this fight we are having right now and it drives a wedge between us, like it already is."

"Andie, nothing could drive me away from you."

"You just ran, Eli, we started fighting and you ran from me instead of staying to hash it out. What happens if we try to have a baby and it doesn't happen are you going to run then?"

Eli took a deep breath. "No, I just didn't want to yell at you, I wanted to be calmer to have this conversation, just please let's start over. I love you, we don't have to talk about it anymore today, when we get over everything else we can reexamine this possibility okay?"

"Just don't run from me again, I never back down from you, remember? I stood up to you when we were dealing with Lily, why would you think I wouldn't do it now?"

"I didn't want you to have to, because I'm a fucking moron, just come on let's go back home."

She let him lead her back to the horse and help her up on it then he got back onto Lightning. When they got back to the barn Dale took the horses and they headed back into the house. He kept her close to him again.

When they got inside the girls were up, Eli paid Belle and she left. Andie and Eli played with the girls until it was time for them to start supper for themselves and the girls. They gave the girls their baths and put them to bed and they went to bed but they were still too tense to do anything but hold each other all night.

They both hoped that in the next couple of days their tension and the fight between them would fade and things could get back to normal, back to completely involved in each other and loving each other.

Chapter 20

Andie rolled to find the warmth that should have been beside her, her eyes flew open when she didn't find it. She looked at the clock, it was only midnight. Maybe he went to the bathroom? She stared at the ceiling for another fifteen minutes before she finally got up to go search for Eli.

She checked the girls' room first, they both were sawing logs. A small smile touched her lips and she pulled the door closed to a crack. She made her way down the hall trying to hear any sign of Eli.

Nothing.

Where was he? She wrapped her arms around herself a little. She walked into the living room, Eli was asleep on the couch. One foot propped up on the arm of the couch, his other leg stretched out off the couch, the heel of his foot resting against the floor. He had an arm draped over his eyes.

She let out a sigh, he looked so smushed. She made her way over to him, she moved closer when her foot landed on something sharp. She let out a yelp and stumbled forward, landing on top of Eli.

The next thing she knew she was pushed back onto the

couch, her hands pinned above her head and Eli's muscular body was pressed against her.

"Andie, what are you doing?" he rasped out as his breath settled down a little.

"I came to find you, what are you doing?"

"Nothing."

"Then come to bed, Eli, please?"

He huffed a little and slowly pulled away, he helped her up and knocked the toy she had stepped on out of the way, then led her down the hallway to their room. He lay down, then pulled her down on top of him. He kissed her forehead and wrapped his arms around her. "Go back to sleep, baby, I love you."

"I love you too," she answered sleepily as she snuggled against him, he still felt so tense beneath her but she couldn't keep her eyes open.

Eli held Andie close to him and rubbed her back gently. He stared up at the ceiling. He brushed her soft hair from her face gently. He was glad she didn't press him anymore about why he'd been out on the couch. Asleep none the less.

He was trying his damnedest to protect his family. When he got the phone call from Levi about seeing someone on the property his stomach had dropped. His plan had been to stay awake to make sure nothing happened or that he could spot the person Levi had seen.

But, no. His stupid ass fell asleep on that uncomfortable couch. He ran his fingers through her long, silky, soft hair again and kissed her cheek. He had to keep his girls safe.

Andie let out a whimper as she tried to move closer to him.

"Shh, I'm right here," he whispered as he rubbed her back

again. And today she was supposed to help Bruce and Rose unpack. Why did he ever agree to it?

He began to fall asleep too.

Andie jerked awake when Lily began to cry. She crawled over Eli and rushed to the girls. She picked Lily up and began to change her and sat her down with some toys then proceeded to do the same with Lucy.

She took them out to the kitchen and put them in their highchairs. She began to get their baby food ready, at the pop of the lid the strawberry-banana smell wafted to her nose and she felt her stomach roil, she set the jar on the counter. "Eli!" she yelled as she rushed out of the kitchen.

Eli came rushing out of the bedroom. "What's the matter?"

"The girls are in their chairs, can you... please?" She rushed into the bathroom and began to get sick. She finally could relax a little. Tears ran down her cheeks, and her throat hurt a little bit.

She leaned against the tub trying to settle her gasping. She shuddered a little, she must have eaten something bad. She was okay though, she had to be, she had to help Rose and Bruce today while Belle came to watch the girls. She slowly stood up, pushing the shaking feeling away as she moved to the white sink.

She turned on the water, splashing some on her face then brushed her teeth. She ran a hand over her face trying to compose herself then headed back to the kitchen.

Embarrassment swarmed over her as Eli looked at her. She tried to walk around him but he stuck out his arm and pulled her down into his lap and they finished feeding the girls.

Eli gave the girls their bottles and wrapped an arm around Andie's waist when she tried to get up, he pressed his other hand against her forehead and cheeks gently. "You look a little flushed, baby, are you okay?"

"Um, yeah, I'm fine, so what are you doing today?"

"Well, I guess I'm actually going to help the guys out today since I've been slacking because of a particular woman that I love."

She smiled faintly, "I'm sorry."

"Oh, I'm not complaining." He kissed the back of her neck. "Belle will be here soon, guess we better get ready."

"Yeah, I guess so." She got out of his lap and grabbed the girls. Eli went to follow her but she called out, "I've got it, Eli." She rushed out of the kitchen and to the nursery and began to get the girls cleaned up and dressed.

Eli stood there unable to say anything. He put the spoons, trays, and bottles in the sink to be washed up. Andie was acting very strange today. He started the water and began to clean up.

Once he was done he found Andie with the girls sitting on the bed. He lay down by them and they began to crawl all over him. He held them close as Andie changed into a blue tank top and a pair of cut-off jean shorts. She tried to snap them but couldn't.

She let out a huff and stripped them off. "I told you not letting me do anything was causing me to gain weight."

He smiled at her, his woman, and said, "Well, if you have, it doesn't look like it to me, I think you look great." Just then Lucy grabbed his nose and said Da da again. "How about Mama?"

"Ma," she squealed making Andie turn around quickly.

He smiled up at Andie as she climbed onto the bed and Lucy reached out to her. Eli grabbed Lily and sat her on his chest as Andie hugged Lucy. "Baby, why don't you just stay home with us like this all day?"

"Maybe tomorrow? We already arranged for Belle to come over, so we should stick to the plan and it'll be good to see Rose and Bruce. I was also thinking we could invite them and your parents for supper tonight."

He adjusted Lily and sat up a little, he brushed his knuckles against Andie's cheek brushing some hair from her flushed cheeks, "Only if you're sure."

"Yeah, why not? We can do something simple, get some pizzas."

"All right, babe." He leaned over and kissed her. "Why don't you finish getting dressed, then I will. We'll wait for Belle, and while we wait we'll play with the girls."

"Okay." She smiled and kissed him again but he felt like she was holding back a little. He let it go and she got dressed. She took the kids out to the living room while he got dressed, what could possibly be going through her mind? She was pulling away a little and he didn't know why. He loved her, so they'd had an argument, it's what couples did, not everything was going to be sunshine and roses. But she knew that better than anyone else he knew. He dressed and headed out to the living room and found her playing with both of the girls.

He sat down and joined in for a while until Belle finally showed up. They told her what they'd done so far and how their moods were and headed outside after he set the alarm. Eli walked Andie to her car. She went to get in but he pulled her back to him. "Baby, are you sure you're okay?"

"Yeah, I'm fine, really." She wrapped her arms around him slightly, and he bent down to kiss her passionately.

"All right, babe, if anything happens you let me know, okay? I'll be there in a flash."

"I know, thank you," she whispered and got into the car.

Eli watched Andie leave down the driveway and he headed

to the barn, there was something she was getting scared about and he couldn't get her to tell him, it was going to drive him mad. Why couldn't he get her to understand she didn't have to be alone anymore, that he was going to be beside her. He shook his head and headed into the barn. She just needed time.

Andie sat in the parking lot of the store, this was impossible, she'd been told she couldn't have a kid and then she was told she couldn't have anymore. And now she was late. This made no sense, she tried to convince herself it was just the stress of everything that was happening. But there was one way she could be sure without going to a doctor, who would probably look at her like she was crazy given her prior diagnosis.

She glanced around, she was so glad Eli let her go on her own to Rose and Bruce's new home, it was the only way she was going to get away with this and not give him any false hope. As soon as she walked into the store she made a beeline to the tests and stared. So many thoughts flashed through her mind. What if she wasn't? Would she be disappointed? Would she be relieved? Would she have another chance to mother another child? How would Eli feel? Excited or upset? She chewed on her lip as she stared at all the tests that lined the wall. Who knew there could be so many stupid tests for the same thing?

She reached out and grabbed the test she had taken when she had been pregnant with Lucy. She rushed to the check-out, paid, and left quickly. Her heart was beating out of her chest, it was almost painful. She didn't know why she was so worked up, this wasn't the first time she took a test, but there was so much more at stake this time, at least before she knew where she stood with the man who got her pregnant. She made her way to her house, went inside and hurried to the bathroom.

She began to rip open the package and foil, and kept telling herself to expect a not pregnant, because all of this was just stress. Then again what if she was taking the stupid test too early? She just wanted her brain to shut up. She began to take the test and closed the cap and laid it on the sink. She finished, dressed, and waited. She sat on the edge of the tub as her legs bounced with nerves.

Enough time had passed and she picked up the test, she pulled her phone out and took a picture of the word staring back at her. She couldn't believe this. She called Eli and said, "We need to talk."

"Hey, what's wrong?"

"Nothing, I just know we have to talk. I'm going to send you a picture."

"Okay." He drew out the word sounding a little scared.

She pulled up the picture, sent it to him, put the phone back up to her ear and started talking. "Eli, I don't expect anything. I hope you know that. I know we've said we love each other and I do love you, Eli, so much. I'm sorry about my mood this morning, and I'm sorry I got sick and everything that's been going on, this couldn't be a worse time for this but I need you to know."

"Baby, breathe," he said huskily.

"I'm trying."

"Just give me a minute."

She closed her eyes tightly as she waited for Eli to look at the picture. She heard some rustling and then she heard his voice.

"Marry me."

She opened her eyes quickly. "I'm sorry, what?"

"Marry me," he repeated.

"Wait, why?"

"Because it makes sense. You know this. I know this. Hell, those two little girls probably even know, so marry me."

"This isn't just because of the picture I sent you, is it?"

"No, of course not, just helps some."

"I'm not getting married because of the situation. I'm not weak. I don't need to be married to have a baby, I already had one."

"Baby, we're having a baby, not just you. I know you're so strong. I want to marry you because I love you, this just gives us more of a reason to hurry and make our life together."

"I don't know, Eli. I just... I think I need some time to think. I have to go before Rose and Bruce get home."

"Wait, where are you?"

"My house," she answered slowly.

"Are you serious, Andie?"

"Yes, I didn't know where else to take the test, I'm sorry, Eli." She closed her eyes as she heard a huff.

"Okay, listen to me. Make sure no one is around, get to your car and leave. Go straight to Rose and Bruce's, just make sure no one is following you."

"I will, Eli. I promise. I love you."

"I love you too, but we're going to talk about this later."

Andie did exactly what Eli said after they got off the phone, no need to borrow anymore trouble. Her eyes darted around as she went to her car. She got in quickly and sat there for a minute and stared at her house.

Marriage? She just showed him she was indeed having their baby and he asked her to marry him over the phone? She took a deep breath and started her car, then cautiously made her way to Bruce and Rose's new home. Watching for anyone following her on the way.

She made it safely and headed to the door. She knocked softly, she kept glancing around her. The door finally opened and she was assaulted with a horrible, pungent floral smell. She covered her mouth and nose quickly.

"Andie! It's so good to see you!" Rose Howell exclaimed in excitement.

"I'm sorry, can I use your bathroom for a minute?" she asked, her mouth and nose still covered by her hand.

"Sure, are you okay?"

"Um, yeah, bathroom?" She didn't know how much longer she was going to be able to hold out.

Rose showed her the bathroom and Andie rushed in and began to get sick again.

"Andie?" Rose went in and held her hair back a little. "Are you okay?"

"Yeah, I'm fine, just a tiny bit under the weather. I'm sorry." She didn't want anyone but Eli to know in case this was just some stupid fluke.

"Sweetheart, why don't you go home and get some rest?"

"But I really wanted to help."

"It's okay, sweetie, your health is more important, especially since you have the girls now."

"I'm really sorry, Mrs. Howell. We also wanted to have you and the Camerons over for pizza tonight. Can we go ahead and plan that so you and Mr. Howell can see Lily? If I'm not feeling any better we can plan for another time."

"Okay, that sounds good, we'll see you later, dear."

Andie felt like such a failure. She headed to her car. She grabbed a handful of breath mints and ate them as she headed home. She didn't want to deal with Belle but didn't know where Eli would be.

Eli was sitting in the saddle lecturing himself. He was a moron, she sent him the picture with the test and the word pregnant in the window and he asked her to marry him, over the phone? What was wrong with him?

Dale rode up to him. "Well, don't you look thrilled?"

"Huh, what?" Eli jerked his gaze to his main ranch hand.

"You look like you're going to be sick." He stopped his horse beside Eli's.

"Oh, Andie's pregnant."

"Oh." His brow puckered a little.

"No, I'm excited about it, but I just… I asked her to marry me."

"I'm sorry, what? Where is she?"

"I asked her over the phone. God, I'm an idiot."

Dale choked back a laugh. "Well, you could always try again."

"I'm going to have to, I guess." He jerked his head up when he thought he heard the sound of an alarm but it disappeared just as quickly. He shook his head a little as he stared over the rolling hills of his land, how was he going to make up for his stupid proposal over the phone? What was wrong with him? That was the least romantic way to purpose, ever.

Something suddenly settled in his stomach and it wasn't good. He pulled out his phone and began to dial Levi. He was supposed to be watching the house, hopefully, nothing was going on there and nothing was happening to Andie.

She took a deep breath as she pulled into the driveway by Eli's truck. Just as she parked the car, she glanced around, there was no sign of Levi and she wondered where he was. Surely Eli would have had him posted again. She had just stepped out of the car and was headed toward the house when the alarm began to go off. She rushed up the steps, stumbling a little, as she flew into the house and shut off the alarm quickly. She heard the girls crying loudly and a loud scream, it sounded like it had come from the kitchen. "Belle!"

She ran down the hallway getting closer to the sound of the girls, she froze when her eyes landed on the terrifying scene. She swallowed hard as she took in Belle's scared look, someone in a mask holding her around the neck with a gun pressed to her head. It was him. Had to be. "Let her go." Andie tried to move closer.

"One more step and she dies, have you got the money?"

"No, I haven't and I'm not going to. You are not controlling this family! You already took two people away from it, wasn't that enough?"

"What?"

"You killed Candice and Caleb, your bullets matched the bullets that killed them, you were sloppy just not sloppy enough until now. Let her go, she's got nothing to do with this. It's me you want, just leave the woman and the girls alone. You want me dead? Well here's your chance." She glared at the masked man, how dare he pretend to not know what she was talking about. She didn't know whether to try to make him angry or calm him down. She certainly was neither one. This asshole killed her best friend, her husband, and now was trying to use their little girl and Eli for his own gain.

"I want to know what happened that night. She was my best friend, I have a right to know. Why did you do it?" She moved a little closer hoping the man didn't notice. She had to get him away from the girls and Belle.

"Andie, watch out!"

She went to turn but a fist slammed into her face hard. "It wasn't him who did it. It was me," the voice said. She looked up but his face was covered in a mask too, but she knew that voice. That cynical voice had tormented her while beating her within an inch of her life and here he was again, only this time she wasn't letting him get the chance to possibly hurt her, or any of her babies, all three of them.

She glared at him. "Why did you do it, Daryl?" she demanded.

He snatched her up by the hair. "Actually, that was just a lucky accident. I just needed some money while on my way to Arizona, they were out late, I didn't expect the man to put up a fight, but he did and hey, it cost both of them."

She kicked him in the shin hard and slammed her fist into his nose. "You are an asshole, I hate you, you knew it was Candice."

He slapped her hard, making her head whip backward. "No, bitch, actually I didn't, you know how long it had been since I'd seen that woman? But apparently, they both deserved it since they took you away from me."

"Shut up, Daryl," the other masked man's angry voice demanded.

Andie looked from one to the other. "Just let the girls and Belle go, it's me you both want, let them go," she pleaded. She could probably handle one of them but not both of them, she was in trouble and she had no idea what to do. "What did you do to Levi?"

"Ha, that big, bearded man? Smashed him over the head, came right up behind him and *wham*," Daryl answered. "He wasn't too bright."

She let out a breath at least no one else died, unless they'd hit him hard enough to cause his death. Her heart pounded, her throat began to close in a panic, what to do, what to do?

Eli began to panic. "Dale, Levi didn't answer his phone, Belle's not either, come on."

The men rushed back to the house and Eli began to call

Andie's phone, she didn't pick up either. Fuck. Something was wrong, very wrong. His heart leaped in his chest as he saw Andie's car parked by his truck.

"Dale, go to the barn and get the rest of the hands, tell them to come armed, something's not right," he instructed and watched the man go into the barn. He was so angry and confused, where was Levi? He heard a groan come from the side of the house, he rushed over and saw the big man lying on the ground. He dialed the cops and told them what was possibly going on. He knelt beside Levi and tried to talk to him but he was too out of it to be any help. He cursed some more and went to go inside when he heard the yelling. His stomach bottomed out. No. No. No.

"Just let Belle leave, let her take the girls and leave. Let them leave first then you get me, you both want revenge, apparently. What better way to get it then to take me?" Andie knew this wasn't going to work. "Hell, I only know who one of you are, so what does it matter and she has no clue who either one of you are, just let them go."

The masked man who was holding Belle glared at her. She had to plan this just right, she had to get away from Daryl, tackle the other man and get the gun away from Belle at the same time and pray it didn't go off and hit one of the girls. She tried to stay calm.

"You know she's right, man. We could just let the woman go, let the one kid go, I mean I don't have a claim to that one and I don't want her."

"But you don't know which one is yours," Andie reminded Daryl. "If either one of them is yours, you beat me pretty bad that night, Daryl, who says I didn't lose it or there was something wrong with the child. I mean, it was your sperm who impregnated me, you're not the brightest."

That earned her a harsh slap that knocked her down but sent her skidding across the floor, and she was now closer to Belle and the other man. It had to be Tame, she didn't know who else would want this to happen besides his stupid, drunk, drug-impaired ass. She waited until Daryl came close to her and she shoved her foot up against him and hit just the right spot. He curled into a ball and held himself while Andie sprung to her feet and jerked the other man's gun hand away from Belle.

"Belle, run, get the girls and go, now, please!" she yelled as she struggled with man number two. She shoved the man back further from Belle and the girls. She kept an eye on them and Belle did as she said. She grabbed both girls and ran.

Andie got the gun slammed into her and she momentarily lost her balance and the man aimed at Belle. "No!" Andie got up and shoved the man's arm away and shoved him out the sliding glass door in the kitchen as the gun went off deafening her again.

Eli couldn't mistake that sound, that was a gunshot, he shoved the door open and started to run in when Belle came running out with both girls. He caught her quickly. "What's going on?"

"Andie's in there with two men," she answered in a rush, trying to catch her breath.

"What?" he looked to Dale who was coming up to them now. He watched Dale throw his arms around Belle and speak to her soothingly.

Eli kissed his baby girls and headed into the house, not caring anymore. He heard the sirens coming but they were still a little too far away. He rushed down the hall to the kitchen and saw one man curled in the fetal position. "Dale, get someone in here with rope!" he called over his shoulder.

He saw the sliding glass door was shattered. He took a deep breath when he heard the grunts and pants of breath. He rushed to the broken door when one of his other hands came in and tied the first guy up. He saw Andie struggling with the guy who had a gun again. He cursed and didn't know what to do, she was too precious to put in harm's way to get the man off of her.

He walked out onto the deck and started towards the man to get him off of Andie. Suddenly the man stood up and pulled Andie in front of him again shoving the gun against her head. Eli's mouth dried at the thought of this man putting his woman and their children in harm's way. He balled his hand into a fist before he pointed his own gun at the masked man.

Andie gripped the arm around her throat and tried to pull it away from her. This wasn't good. Eli was going to get hurt if she didn't do something. She made eye contact with him and mouthed 'I love you' right before she slammed her elbow into the man's stomach and stomped on his foot hard. He jerked back and away from Andie just enough but didn't let her go yet.

She tried to pull away from him but he held her wrist tightly.

She screamed and slammed her fist into his nose, she was hit with the gun knocking her down but the man let go of her.

She then heard two gunshots, the guy stumbled back a little and then fell to his knees beside her. She moved away from him, the blood making her nauseous and she screamed. She then felt a pair of arms wrap around her and lift her up from the deck. She screamed again but then heard the unmistakable voice and she turned her head to face him. "Eli," she sobbed out and she moved into his arms and wrapped her arms and legs around him.

He moved further away from the body as he held onto her tightly just as Carl and Dean ran onto the deck.

Everything else seemed to move in a blur, she explained her half of everything, and Daryl ended up confessing to everything and admitting they had begun to look for Andie, but they just stumbled onto the town and he did kill Candice and Caleb. Andie had to hold onto Eli tightly before he would have gone and broken Daryl's nose, not that he didn't deserve it, but she needed him now more than ever to keep calm and be there for her and the girls and the baby they had made.

She couldn't believe both terrible men from her past had teamed up and were sick enough to come after her. But it was all over now.

Finally, everyone left and they were able to clean up. Eli managed to put some plastic up over the door which would more than likely be replaced the next day. Eli made Andie cancel the dinner with his parents and the Howells due to everything that happened. He just wanted her and the girls.

They had eaten a little pizza and they were in the living room where Eli didn't let go of any of them. "Don't ever do that again," he said sternly.

"I'm sorry, I just knew I had to get Belle out of the way and the girls, they had nothing to do with it, it was me they wanted."

"I know, you did a great job today, baby. I love you but don't ever scare me like that again. We still need to have a talk though," he whispered against her ear. She was sitting in his lap leaning back against the couch arm, Lucy was snuggled against him and Lily was snuggled against her.

She locked eyes with him. "What about?"

"We'll discuss *that* later. More importantly, will you marry me? I'll go get you a ring tomorrow, but I've known for a while I don't want to ever be without you. I love you so much and I want us to be a real family. I want to be Lily's dad, Lucy's dad, I want to be your husband."

"Not just because of the baby?"

"No, not just because of the baby, I want you in my life forever. I promise from this day forward I will love you and cherish you and take care of you and our two girls and whatever we have, hopefully, a boy, I am a little outnumbered," he chuckled as he laid his hand against her stomach.

"So, would you have asked me to marry you even if I wasn't pregnant?"

"Of course, you complement me so well, keep me calm, I could have killed that fucker tonight and not thought twice about it, but instead you let me hold onto you to keep me from doing something so stupid, he'll get what he deserves. I should have and would have killed them both but you kept me from doing that, I need you in my life forever, Andrea Nicole Malone, now are you marrying me or not?"

"Yes, Elijah Joseph Cameron, I will. I love you."

They kissed each other passionately and they cuddled there on the couch for a little while. Andie perked up a little bit and said, "So we are going to have a nineteen-month-old, a seventeen-month-old and a newborn, all at the same time. God, I think we may need some help."

"Eh, we'll handle it, baby, one day at a time."

She snuggled into Eli as they held the girls and he held her also. She had never felt so safe in her entire life. Eli promised he would always protect her, even from herself, disciplining her when he felt it was called for and she knew she had a lesson coming. She wouldn't have it any other way. She slowly began to fall asleep in his arms as he pressed his lips to her forehead. It had been such a crazy, long day.

Epilogue

ndrea Malone and Lucy Malone were officially Camerons. She had walked down the aisle to her husband alone but that was okay. Neither one of them had a best man or maid of honor in honor of those they lost. Her bakery was officially painted powder blue.

Belle had managed to tell everyone how Andie had saved her. People had changed a little bit but no one would ever be able to replace Candice. She was four months along now.

As the girls played on the blanket, she'd spread out on the front porch, she was in the swing rubbing her bump. They had found out they were going to have a baby boy, they'd picked out the name Joseph Caleb Cameron. She smiled as she rubbed her bump and the girls played.

So much had changed over the last five months, two daughters, one very amazing, devoted husband, and a son on the way, an uncle and aunt gone and a mother and father but Eli and she were moving on with their lives. Their love was growing stronger by the day. The trust and security she never had in her life before was overflowing from her life now. Eli tended to be overprotective, her sore bottom could attest to that, but she had never felt so safe and loved ever. They'd made the change to the doorway Eli had wanted to do with the master bedroom and guest room and bathroom.

But they'd kept the other bedroom the same to keep Candice and Caleb's memory alive.

She glanced up when she saw the black, tinted-window car coming up the driveway. She almost panicked but she knew she was safe now.

The car parked closer to the house than was probably necessary. She slowly got up out of the swing and walked to the steps of the porch, wrapping her hands around the banister. She looked back to the girls who were still playing, then she turned back to the car just as Caleb and Candice's lawyer got out.

"Mrs. Cameron." He held a hand out to her when he got closer to her. She shook it and then he handed her a manila envelope. She took it as her eyebrows raised. "I was instructed to hold on to those until your wedding day to Eli, there's one for you and one for him as well, congratulations, Andrea, on the marriage and another baby."

"Thank you, sir."

"Well, I'll leave you to read your letter." He turned to walk back to his car as Eli came up over a hill on his horse, Lightning.

The lawyer left and Eli came up to the house, he pulled Lightning to a stop and got off quickly. He raced up the steps, wrapping his strong, comforting arms around Andie, "What's going on, everything okay?"

She opened the envelope and pulled out the two regular envelopes. One was addressed to her the other to Eli. She looked up at him. "This is Candice's writing," she whispered.

"That's Caleb's," he said and took the other envelope addressed to him. "Hey, you're supposed to be resting, come on." He picked her up and took her over to the swing.

Lucy stood up and held her little hands up to Eli, he picked both girls up and sat them on the swing between them.

Andie glanced at Eli. "They wrote us letters?"

"I guess so." He breathed out.

Andie opened hers first.

If you're reading this, Andie, then something happened to me and Caleb but then it also means you and Eli are happy together and finally married. I'm so sorry we missed it but we love you so much. I'm sorry if he was mad at you when he first found out about our arrangement for Lily. But we did it because we knew that would probably be the only way he'd open his eyes and shirk the stubbornness he has. The other reason was we knew you'd protect Lily so well because you never had that protection. We also knew how much Lily meant to you. I don't know when or what age you have her but just make a promise to love her forever, no matter how hard things get. Tell her how much we loved her and that we hate everything that we've missed and will continue to miss. She can call you mom and call Eli dad, because, of course, she'll need those in her life. You know how cruel this world can be and you'll know what not to do when it comes to loving her, protecting her, and how to care for her. I'm so happy you are finally a part of a family again. You always were my sister and now Lily will have a sister in Lucy. Caleb and I love you so much and appreciate everything you've done for our little girl. I hope you didn't have to wait too long for Eli to come around. I'm sorry you had to go it alone but you did fine I'm sure. There may be some fights along the way but now you'll have the love and protection you deserve.

Love always,
Candice.

Andie took a deep breath as she looked from her best friend's signature to the girls then to Eli. She fought the tears as they switched letters and she began to read Caleb's letter to Eli.

. . .

Hey bone head, congratulations on the family, and the marriage. Sorry I couldn't be there and sorry it was such a drastic measure to get you to finally realize you could love and be the best for Andie. I tried so many times to try to get you to wake up and see how good you two would be for each other, she was ready to be yours at our wedding but you being the stubborn man that you are wouldn't open your eyes and wouldn't do it. I'm glad you finally have, I hope you realize how much she's gone through already and how strong she is. She will love you to the ends of the earth and don't ever take advantage of that. Worship her every day and never be harsh with her. I don't know how much she's told you but she deserves to be cared for, loved gently, and made happy every day. I'm sorry Candice and I are gone but please keep our memory alive for Lily pad. I love you, little brother, even if you needed this hard push to fall for Andie but I'm glad you did.

Caleb.

"So they totally had this planned, huh?" Eli whispered.

"I guess so."

"Well, I'm glad they did. I love you, Andie, and both our girls and our little boy." He laid his hand on her baby bump and leaned forward to kiss her.

Too bad Candice and Caleb were gone. But they would do right by them where Lily was concerned, it still wasn't fair, but they'd keep their memory going just for her. And they would always make sure their girls and boy knew how much they were loved. Always and forever.

The End

Blushing Books

Blushing Books is one of the oldest eBook publishers on the web. We've been running websites that publish spanking and BDSM related romance and erotica since 1999, and we have been selling eBooks since 2003. We hope you'll check out our hundreds of offerings at http://www.blushingbooks.com.

Blushing Books Newsletter

Please join the Blushing Books newsletter
to receive updates & special promotional offers.
You can also join by using your mobile phone:
Just text BLUSHING to 22828.